# Verucca Victorious

## S. L. Wideman

## Other books by S. L. Wideman

### Space Station Olympus Series
Iona
Kore (coming soon)

### Non-series Books
Verucca Victorious
Forbidden Magic (coming soon)

# Chapter One

The first thing I noticed, even before I opened my eyes, was how soft the bed felt. It was like laying on a cloud, wrapped in satin sheets and down feather pillows. This was new.

I slowly opened my eyes, taking in everything as it came into focus. The plain white ceiling offered no clues, and neither did the dark navy blue walls. My black wood bed was covered by the most beautiful set of royal blue and black sheets. Two doors were on the wall to my left, probably the closet and bathroom, and the door on the opposing wall led out of the room. The remaining furniture in the room matched the bed's black wood and was not what I would consider feminine except for a tiny vanity across the bed, littered with multicolored bottles of perfumes and lotions. Pictures adorned each wall and I could see they were mostly from newspapers. It was an elegant room, the grandest I've woken up in outside of fairy tales.

I stretched, allowing new memories to fill me in this incunabulum period of my new life. I knew who I used to be before I was snatched up by an Author and plopped into a Story. I was a Character, a person created to only exist for the whims of an Author. Just moments before I was on my way to talk at the *All the Time Villains* meeting and reconnecting with a character from my past. Drake Cavendash, aka Prince Todd McHottie from one of my first Stories, ran into me and invited me out to coffee. He was the first to ever want to see me after the Story ended. In my life, I played the evil stepmother, greedy orphanage director, and wicked witch. So, waking to find myself in the lap of luxury was a pleasant change of pace.

Who I was before didn't matter. I was now Verucca Tottenstinker. Though an unfortunate name, I appeared to have done alright for myself. I slid out of bed, sifting cautiously through my new knowledge. Everything was, indeed, mine: My soft bed, my fancy apartment in Faycrest city, and my wonderful new life. The news clippings on the walls helped me discover the memories of my new persona. They showed me to be a successful business woman with many awards. Here was an article of my being named Business Woman of the Year, and here was another that talked about my charitable contributions. I was dating a handsome and successful CEO of one of the biggest companies in the city.

I quickly shifted through my memories, hunting any grain of ill intent. For once, I found none. Neither my boyfriend nor I had any children I could abuse. While I subscribed to no religion, I was not some crazy cultist or evil witch holding my boyfriend through the dark arts. I made all my own money and was active in several benefiting charities.

My heart skipped a beat and a real smile lit my face. I was not the villain! There was nothing evil about me! Could this Story finally be my Happily Ever After, my one chance at redemption for years of playing the cardboard bad guy?

With that cheerful thought, I explored my new surroundings. As Verucca, my style was both elegant and practical. Still ugly as sin, I proved one did not have to be beautiful to be successful. My designer suit didn't hang off my thin form and it nicely masked my knobby knees and elbows. I was not pretty, a fact I was all too aware of, with a body of skin-and-bones, pallid skin, beady eyes, a large hooked nose, and shoulder-length stringy black hair. My looks were the reason I was often Called to play witches in Stories. But, now dressed in good clothes, I looked half-way decent.

My apartment was colossal! The master suite was situated in a loft with a private veranda which had a hot tub, a large master bath, and walk-in closet that could double as a second apartment. The main portion of the apartment sat at the bottom of an elegant glass and steel spiral stairway. There was another private veranda with an area for sunbathing and BBQs, a spacious kitchen and dining room that opened up to a generous living room. There was a powder room and a private office and nearly every wall faced the outside world with floor-to-ceiling windows. Pictures and sculptures of cats were everywhere, and an adorable black kitten greeted me with a happy purr.

I scooped the kitten up as I continued through the apartment. "Look Diamond, all of this is ours," I said as the name of the kitten came to me. "This is our chair. This is our fireplace. There is our little inglenook by the fireplace. Oh, Diamond, I can't wait to read books, all tucked away back there. This is our … well, my cup. You can't have coffee. Speaking of which, I should make some."

Humming happily, I took Diamond to the kitchen and looked around for a coffee machine. As I bent to look under the cabinet, I felt the presence of Author finally looking in on me. Officially, the Story had begun.

Behind me came a discreet cough. Turning, I found myself facing a young man dressed in a bright neon pink shirt and simple black pants. His neon yellow hair was spiked up fashionably and a crystal stud blinked merrily in his left ear. He held up a large cup of coffee and the morning paper, his perfectly plucked eyebrows inching up as he made his offering.

"Uh, yes, hello?" What was I supposed to do? There was no guidance from Author, no tugging on my strings to make me perform.

"Morning Ms. Tottenstinker," the boy said in a sing-song voice. "Your morning paper and coffee. We have a busy day, darling." He walked over to the kitchen table with a swish in his step any girl would kill for and placed the paper and coffee down. "I'll take care of Diamond for you, Ms. Tottenstinker."

"Uh, thank you." I struggled with his name, but none was coming to me. He must be important if he was showing up this early, so why didn't I have access to his name?

He either saw my confusion or was prompted by Author. "It's Steven, Ms. Tottenstinker."

"Right, Steven. So, let's get started." I handed Diamond over to him, who started purring again, and picked up my coffee. As I enjoyed the slightly bitter taste and swirl of faint flavoring, I watched him feed the cat. Taken by a sudden direction, I grabbed a pen and piece of paper and started jotting down notes. I sipped my coffee and, in between sips, wrote.

"Steven, what coffee is this?"

"I know you're not a huge fan of the flavored stuff, Ms. Tottenstinker, but it's a new strawberry flavor at the little no name cafe down the street. Everyone is raving about it, so I thought you should try it."

I took another sip. "It's not bad. A little too subtle if you ask me." Looking at my notes, I realized they were all about coffee. The texture and flavor, ideas for names, and a list of fruits. It came to me that I was the CEO of a successful coffee business and this was our morning routine. Steven brings me coffee to keep up on my competitors and I figure a way to make the coffee better.

Rereading my notes, I frown slightly. If I owned a coffee business, why did my notes also pertain to cats? What would "Siamese dark roast with a hint of mint and strawberry, splash of balsamic" have to do with this set up?

"There are some interesting articles in the paper, Ms. Tottenstinker."

Taking his direction, I glanced through the paper. I participated in many Stories, but this was the first one to have a welcome letter. No clue as to the plot, just a generic 'let's have fun'. As I read the paper, I felt as if a huge weight was lifted from my shoulders as Author moved on to oversee another part of the Story.

Steven breathed a sigh of relief. "About time. I never like it when Author is watching. I just can't be myself." He dropped dramatically on the kitchen chair.

"This is a Story and we are Characters. We are not ourselves, and that is the point," I said as I picked Diamond back up. "Author's Will is irrefrangible. We must obey."

"Irre what?"

"Irrefrangible. To not be broken."

Steven laughed. "I didn't think you'd have such a big vocabulary. I mean, for someone who believes in giving herself to Author, I thought you'd keep your words to Author's level."

"In the Stories, yes I do. But, I never just sit around and wait for Author to remember me. On my downtime, I try to read as many books as I can. I devour them by the armload.

Nothing that might have anyone I'd know, but non-fiction and dictionaries. I believe in bettering myself."

Steven and I sat there as I finished the last of my coffee, discussing what we knew about our Characters. I was a self-made billionaire and owner of Tabby Pops Coffee, a specialized coffee chain catering exclusively to the rich. Steven was my right-hand man and personal assistant.

"I'm also the token gay guy in this Story," he said, "though I think I should hand in my gay card with this fashion sense. Neon is so last year." He ran his hand through his spiked hair and grinned. "My wife is going to get such a kick out of this when we get back."

"Wife?"

"Yeah. Don't ask me why, but I'm Called to play a lot of gay guys. I'm a straight arrow. She used to think it was funny, but I can tell it's wearing on her. You know, Author is never wrong and all that, so I must secretly be gay." He sighed. "I really do love her."

"I'm sure she understands. It's just hard to see beyond what Author wants sometimes."

"Right, okay." Steven stood up. "You're my boss who overworks and underpays me. I doubt us sitting here and chatting will be a normal thing as per Author, so we better get our rears in gear and enter the Story."

"Maybe this is some kind of *Christmas Carol* Story," I said hopefully. "I go from the draconian Scrooge to a cream-puff after some scary experience and we all live happily ever after."

Steven shrugged. "Maybe. I can't get a feel on this Story just yet. I normally get a feeling a chapter or two in, and all I know now is that I'm part of a puzzle."

"I get a feeling for my part almost from the start," I said. "Though, to be fair, I've partaken in a few with no imagination and can figure it out in seconds. I like the ones that keep me guessing."

We took my private elevator down to the lobby. Outside my extravagant apartment building was my car, my driver standing by an opened door for me. He tipped his hat as Steven and I got in, eager to be out of the cold, winter air. On the way, Steven went through a date book he carried to tell me what appointments I scheduled that day. Everything sounded so important, it was a little intimidating.

Tabby Pops Coffee was actually housed in two buildings. The main office building sat on the South end of the city, nestled among other large office buildings. From that building, I ruled over my empire.

The second building was known as Cat Camp, and was the factory section of my operation. Tabby Pops Coffee was no ordinary coffee business. It was a version of the exclusive civic cat coffee, only I used ordinary house cats to produce my bitter, but highly sought after, coffee to the rich and famous. I named my blends kitschy little titles like "Sexy Siamese Dark Roast" and "Toffee Tabby Delight". According to Author, this little venture made me the reigning queen of the known coffee world.

"Not that I think this would really work," I said. "I know it does with civic cats because of their digestion, but ordinary house cats are different."

Steven shrugged. "It's a Story. If Author wanted us to get around on Pterodactyls and have lasers shooting from our eyes, it'll work somehow."

As we neared the large office building, we could feel

Author watching us once more. The reason being the large crowd of protesters gathering in the front. Signs declaring Tabby Pops Coffee as abusive to animals were waved about as they stymied the traffic flow.

"Driver, take us in the back way," I ordered. The driver nodded and made a sharp right into an entrance to a parking garage. It was pure luck none of the protesters noticed us.

The driver parked the car and Steven and I got out. Keeping an eye out for any of the protesters, we made our way as stealthily as we could to the parking elevator.

"Why do I get the feeling this is a regular occurrence," I whispered.

"I have that same feeling."

At the elevator, two other women stood waiting. I was immediately struck with the realization I recognized them, but their names did not come to mind. Whoever they were, Verucca Tottenstinker met them in the past. On the left was a tall brunette in a bright purple trench coat. She wore a wide-brimmed hat in the same bright purple and large sunglasses. She held a bucket with something red splashed down one side. The other was a blonde wearing a pink jacket with a fake fur collar and jeans with a glittery flower embroidered down the leg. She, too, held a bucket.

"I don't like the looks of this," Steven whispered.

"Ditto. Everything is telling me to run, but I can feel Author prodding me on," I answered. Then, I felt Author sweep over us and my free-will melt away. This was an important scene, and Author did not want us to mess it up.

The blonde turned and saw us. She nudged her partner and my instinct to run flared once more. Instead, I walked against my will closer to the elevator and the two women.

The brunette gave me a once over. "Verucca Tottenstinker, I presume."

"You presume correctly," I said. "Hurry up and state your business. I'm an important person. Steven, don't just stand there! Summon the elevator." I cringed inwardly. I was going to be one of those characters again; cruel and cold and hated.

The brunette sneered. "You haven't changed at all, have you? Look at you! Verucca Tottenstinker, the oppressor of cats and owner of cat slave shops in the disguise of coffee."

"Oh, please. You're one of those petty protesters, aren't you? Listen, little girl, I'm a busy woman. If you really want to complain about how you view my business, talk to my lawyer."

"How can you sleep at night knowing you're abusing millions of cats," the blonde asked. Her voice was light and wispy and grated on my nerves for some reason.

"I sleep satisfactory, thank you." I pushed by them and headed to where Steven was holding the elevator for me.

"Cat killer!" I felt something warm and wet hit my back. I turned to see the blonde's bucket was now empty. Reaching to feel my back, my hand came away bright red with paint.

"Why you little brat," I spat. "This coat cost more than you could ever make in a year! Give me your name! You're going to pay for this!"

"Just add me to the bill, too, Tottenstinker," the brunette said. She threw the contents of her bucket right in my face. I sputtered as the paint covered me. By the time I wiped it out of my eyes, the two women and Author were gone.

"What was that all about," I asked, turning to Steven.

He shrugged. "Welcome to the Story."

# Chapter Two

"That was pretty scary," Steven said as the elevator doors closed. He pushed the button for the top floor and the elevator started to ascend.

"Getting paint thrown on me is not all that scary," I said. "Not unless I develop latent telekinesis powers."

"Man, don't say that. My neighbor was an extra in that Story. He still has nightmares."

I looked down at my ruined coat. "I have a feeling I'm supposed to know them, but nothing was coming up."

"The brunette is Heather Voldenair, a proactive protester who has been on your tail for the past year or so. The two of you butt heads often as she is convinced you abuse your animals," Steven said. "This is not the first time they've ambushed you with paint."

"And the blonde?"

"No idea. She's new, as far as I can remember."

I watched the little numbers over the door light up, one by one, as we traveled up to my office. "How high are we going," I asked.

"I think it's on the top floor. That appears to be the twentieth floor," Steven said. "Listen, I really have to say, I never saw anyone change the way you did when Author took control. Everything changed. I mean, right now you're so nice, but you gave me shivers earlier."

"Yeah, I know that happens," I said. I leaned back against the wall, my eyes on the numbers. "Not too long ago, I was in another Story. Typical for me, I was the evil stepmother.

When Author pulled my strings, I did the most horrible things. Well, this one scene had me beat my stepdaughter and send her to her room without food. When Author moved on, I quickly made her some dinner and grabbed a first aid kit. I tried to undo the damage, but she threw the bowl of soup I brought up in my face. I was a little too convincing."

"How did it end?"

"The father divorced me to be with his one true love and I ended up dying in a car crash while trying to kidnap the daughter. She made it out with no scrapes or anything. Everyone lived happily ever after."

"Man that sucks."

"I learned to deal." I raised one red hand. The paint was starting to dry. "If this is the worst that happens to me, I can live with it."

The elevator doors opened with a merry ding. Steven and I walked out and were greeted by a mass of people. "Welcome Ms. Tottenstinker!"

I stood there, looking like an escapee from a horror Story. "What is going on?"

A balding man with rather rat-like features and a nervous twitch to his right eye stepped forward. "Well, we know that you want us to greet you every morning like you were some lady in a manor. So, we decided to get in the habit. Even if Author isn't overseeing our actions."

"If Author isn't around, you really don't need to do this," I said. "Um, I need to change my clothes."

"You have a shower in your office," the man said. He held out his hand. "I'm Earl, your office manager. Basically, I am your second or third in command, depending on how you view Steven. Or, rather, how Author views Steven. It can vary day to day."

Earl brought me to my office. It was much like my apartment; dark woods and black fabric everywhere. Stylish and Gothic. I not only had a full bathroom, but a closet with a change of clothes. I had a feeling that being attacked by protesters was a nearly daily occurrence.

Once I was cleaned, Earl took me on a quick tour of the office. It was all pretty generic with lots of cubicles and vague job descriptions. People worked in several departments, unsure of what to do day by day. I knew their pain. On the rare occasion I wasn't the villain, I was just like them.

The rest of my morning was in meetings. My first was to talk with my advertising team on a new product design. Then it was with my Cat Camp personnel about ideas for new flavors. My last meeting was with marketing on which brands to push and which ones to pull back.

"With tomorrow being New Years, we should start thinking about the new spring flavors," my head of marketing told me. She was a nice woman who reminded me of myself. "Last year, Ra of the Desert sold admiringly well. The Egyptian Mau cats have rested all winter and I'm sure we can put them back to work."

"Sounds like a plan. And I believe the Siamese are also rested this winter. I am thinking of a dark roast with a hint of mint and goji berries for a new flavor," I said. There were a few agreeable murmurs around the room before we got down to the details. By the time we broke for lunch, I really felt like a powerful CEO.

For lunch, I ate at my desk. Steven, really getting into his role, had my lunch waiting for me. I ate a ham and cheese on rye while reading a few reports placed on my desk. I barely understood what I was reading, but all the graphs said I was doing well.

The phone rang and I heard my front desk secretary answer it. Suddenly, she paged back to me, "Ma'am, Mr. Edwin Van Der Woody III is on the phone for you. Are you available?"

My heart skipped a beat. I knew that name! This was my handsome boyfriend! "Yes, I'm available. Send him on back." I didn't let the phone finish ringing once before I picked it up.

The voice on the other end was velvety smooth. It was the kind of voice that could say anything and it would make you melt. "Verucca? Is that you?"

"Yes, speaking. Edwin, how are you?"

All at once, memories flooded into me. I could remember our chance meeting at a charity auction and the whirlwind romance that followed. We had just gotten back from Christmas in Hawaii for a friend's wedding. He was the CEO of his own company, something with social media. We've dated for over a year. I was deliriously in love and kept a scrapbook and diary filled with dreams about Edwin under my bed.

"I am doing well. I'm calling to confirm our engagement at Ristorante Piu Ricco di Te tonight for the New Year's Eve Ball. You will be on time?"

Steven, ever so quiet, slid my appointment book next to me. I glanced at it to see that a stylist was coming to pretty me up for the event. "Of course I'll be on time, dearest. In fact, my stylist will be here soon."

"Try not to wear black, Verucca. You look like a crow when you do," Edwin said and hung up. I frowned, staring at the phone. This did not go over like a man calling the woman he loved. Indeed, he sounded almost angry. I tried to not think about it. Maybe that was just how Edwin behaved?

My stylist came in and, now with the order to not wear black, Steven had a few dresses sent up. This was my first Story were I was so rich that a designer company sent dresses to me to try out for an evening. I picked out a beautiful garnet red dress and my stylist went to work on my hair and make-up. As she worked, I daydreamed about what kind of Story this could be. The obvious ending was happiness between myself and Edwin. I could see how this could be a remake of *A Christmas Carol*, but I had a feeling it was in the romance genre. Possibly an *Ugly Duckling* scenario where, after a make-over, Edwin realizes it's always been me he loved?

When I looked in the mirror after my stylist was finished, I was amazed. My straight, stringy hair was curled and pinned up in an elegant fashion. My make-up expertly applied and it did a good job at making me look beautiful. I felt like a new woman.

"You'll take his breath away," Steven said. He walked me down to my car and helped me in.

"How will you get home? You rode in with me," I said.

He shrugged. "I'll either find a ride or poof back to my apartment. Go on and have fun."

Ristorante Piu Ricco di Te was one of the most expensive restaurants in Faycrest. Designed with Italian royalty in mind, the restaurant resembled a mini-castle. White marble walls and gold trim could be found in every room, gold and crystal chandeliers hung from the ceiling and every table was set with only the finest china and golden dinnerware. My high heel shoes clacked along the expensive marble floors and noise from various conversations echoed all around me.

"There you are, Verucca. I was waiting." A handsome man came up to me and I just knew this was Edwin. Tall and lean, his skin had that healthy sun-god tan. His bronze-red hair was styled in a way that said both professional and fun with only a few stray strands falling lightly into his blue eyes. His suit was obviously tailored to fit him and I smiled when I noted a dark navy blue handkerchief in his pocket. I gave that to him on our one month anniversary. Edwin Van Der Woody III was every inch the debonair man I expected him to be.

"You're the last person to arrive," Edwin said as he took my arm. "As usual you can't pull yourself away from your cats long enough to care about our date."

I took a quick look at my watch. "I'm ten minutes early, Edwin."

He sniffed and led me into the main room for the party. All around me was the height of Faycrest nobility. Memories flooded in as I recognized several people as my peers. CEOs and lawyers and politicians filled the room in an array of colorful clothes and loud chatter. Had I been myself, I would have shirked this party and found a nice quiet corner to spend the evening. But I was not me, I was Verucca, and this was her element. I was a member of this coterie and I would act like it!

Edwin and I mingled for a few hours, sparingly sipping expensive champagne and eating cute little hors d'oeuvre. As everyone started to gather for the countdown to midnight, Edwin pulled me out to the back patio. The air was a mixture of cold winter and thick with the presence of Author.

"Before we start this scene, I want to get something off my chest," Edwin said. "For one, this is unacceptable. I'm used to being paired with great beauties. This is my first *Beauty and the Beast* Story."

~ 17 ~

His words stung. I wasn't expecting us to be in love in real life, and when we left here for Outer World, we'd probably never talk to each other again. But, to be so cruelly told this was beyond anything I expected. Even in the Stories where I played the evil stepmother, my husband never came out in our first scene to tell me that he thought I was ugly.

"Author knows best," I said. "Maybe she just moves in mysterious ways."

"Extremely mysterious," he said. "Why would Author ever think that I'd be interested in a creature like you?"

"Well, this is a first for me, too." I looked up at the sky and could feel Author growing impatient. "We better do the scene now."

There was a noticeable shift to Edwin. His demeanor changed from supercilious to kind. "Verucca, I brought you out here to ask a dreadfully important question," he said. Inside, I could hear the countdown starting from thirty. Whatever we were going to do, it would happen in half a minute.

"What question is that, Edwin?" I asked. I inwardly winced at the sound of my voice. This was not the amatory tone of a woman in love, but the frigid voice of a heartless lady.

Edwin knelt and my heart sped up. While Author kept me in my place like an ice statue, my soul was jumping for joy. He produced a black velvet box and I nearly yelled, "Yes" before he asked the question.

"Verucca, we've dated for over a year now. And I have decided that I want to spend the rest of my life with you. Will you do the honors of marrying me?" He opened the box to show the gaudiest diamond ring I've ever seen. The marquis-cut stone had to be two karats at least and there were smaller black diamonds on either side on the gold band.

Inside, the countdown was nearly at one. I reached out and took the ring. After sliding it on my finger, I said, "Of course I'll marry you, Edwin."

"Three! Two! One! Happy New Year!" As the people inside cheered and sang *Auld Lang Syne*, Edwin swept me up in a kiss.

# Chapter Three

I couldn't help but feel giddy after such an opening to a Story. Edwin proposed! I was now engaged to a handsome and successful man! Eager to learn all I could of my character's past, I dug out Verucca's secret diaries from under my bed and read all the ones that dealt with Edwin. I heard of him long before we met; the only son of a wealthy rancher and cereal heiress, he started his social media business in high school. A billionaire by twenty, Edwin remained elusive to the dating world. Oh, sure, he dated pretty starlets and models, but never more than a week. I was his first long-term girlfriend.

I sighed, curled up on my bed with Diamond. "It must be love. At least for the characters. See, Diamond, he asked me out like an awkward school boy at a charity ball." I pointed to the page where Verucca wrote in glowing detail that night. "The first dinner seemed to be mostly business, but we continued to date. And now we're engaged. Oh, Diamond, this is just perfect! At long last, my Happily Ever After is just around the corner."

I wanted to scream the news from every rooftop, but Edwin demanded we keep it quiet for now. Near the end of the month was a charity event presented by Edwin, and he said it would be perfect if we announced our engagement then. For the meantime, we were to keep it hush-hush.

I naturally told Steven. As my personal secretary, he should know all the details. We went through my date book for the year and I jotted down a few dates that worked best for me to see what Edwin could do. We scoured over bridal magazines and I started a bride scrapbook of all my favorite ideas.

"I really like the idea of a Christmas wedding," I said as I tore out another picture. "But I also love the rustic colors of the Fall weddings."

"It's your wedding, Verucca. Do what you want," Steven said.

Two nights before the charity ball, Edwin and I finally got together for dinner to discuss the wedding. We met up once again at Ristorante Piu Ricco di Te, and I had the impression this was our favorite restaurant. I arrived early, eager to discuss things with Edwin. I brought my scrapbook so we could go over some ideas.

"Verucca, there you are," Edwin said as I was brought over to the table. "I've already ordered our wine and salads. I was about to order our food since I had no idea when you'd show."

"I'm ten minutes early, Edwin. I thought I beat you coming here," I said. I pulled out my chair to seat myself as the waiter left and Edwin did not bother to stand and help me. I set the scrapbook on the table.

Edwin gave a disdainful snort. "Just so you know, their specials are roast lamb with mint sauce and glazed seasonal vegetables or grass-fed Kobe steak in a wine and mushroom sauce, served with potatoes."

"I'll have the lamb, thank you." I opened the scrapbook. "Now, I've given our wedding a lot of thought. I think it's best if we plan for the ceremony to be in December at the earliest. Everything I've read states at least a year to plan."

"You're not actually thinking of doing all the planning

yourself, are you?" Edwin looked scandalized by the very idea.

"Oh, no. Remember Bambi's wedding? Of course you do, we just got back from that one. Well, her lovely Hawaii wedding was planned by only the best wedding planner around. I'm getting Steven to book us an appointment with Shirley Lovette." I tapped a finger on the scrapbook. "These are just some ideas. I'm sure she'll be able to help us better manage everything."

"I don't want our wedding in Hawaii, Verucca. That was a god-awful affair with an over-the-top ceremony at the top of a volcano! I was worried I'd get heat stroke and fall in."

I wanted to agree. None of my wedding plans had volcanoes in them, but Author held sway. I found myself pouting. "But Edwin, we need to do something that will make Bambi's wedding look like a pauper's ceremony. If not in Hawaii, than something just as grand. That's why we need Shirley. She'll help us plan the biggest and best ceremony ever."

"I don't see what is wrong with a simple church ceremony," Edwin huffed.

Our food arrived, putting talk of the wedding to side for the moment. I had time to reflect on what was happening. Engaged, yes, but I had a feeling that Edwin's "suggestion" of a church wedding was where we were heading. After being the evil stepmother in so many books - often starting off after my own marriage - I dreamed of participating in my wedding. All of my Stories ended with the heroine having a large wedding at a church or palace. I wanted something unique.

"I'll think over my notes," I said, breaking the silence. "I'm sure we can come up with something that would suit both of us. Let's both think of what we want and find a way to meet in the middle with Shirley."

"Sure. Just, don't mention any wedding ideas at the charity ball. It's for my project and I don't want you doing what you always do and try to steal the spotlight."

"Me? Surely you jest. I shall be the paragon of what you wish to present as your future wife."

Edwin finished his meal and left before I was done. To my surprise, the waiter brought me the check. I paid and left the restaurant, spotting my car waiting for me at the end of the block. With the collar of my coat pulled up high against the cold January air, I slowly made my way to my car, thinking over how to get what I wanted within the bounds Author set for me.

"Hey Tottenstinker!"

I looked toward the sound of someone calling my name as I passed an alley. An object was thrown at me and I instinctively dropped my book to catch it. A bright flash went off, blinding me for a moment and I heard people around me ask what was going on. As the light faded and the dark spots started to go away, I looked at what I now held in my arms.

"Oh my God!" I dropped the package on the ground and a dead cat tumbled out. Someone screamed and I heard people yelling for the police. My driver got out of my car and ran up to me.

"Ma'am, I think we should leave," he said. He grabbed my scrapbook and pulled me along. I barely paid him any mind, my gaze glued to the cat. It looked like Diamond. Who would do such a thing?

# Chapter Four

I awoke the next morning feeling ill at ease. The image of that poor cat was still burned in my mind. I could only thank my lucky stars that it was not, in fact, really Diamond. My poor kitty spent the night hugged to my chest. I knew I would have to put up with some abuse; no path to Happily Ever After was ever easy.

I slid out of bed and Diamond, freed from my grasp, ran out of my room in a hurry. Sluggishly, I tried to keep up with my normal morning routine. A shower helped me feel more human and I went downstairs to find breakfast. Steven was already sitting in my kitchen with my usual offering of coffee and newspaper.

"We have a problem," he said, pushing the paper my way.

Cautiously, I opened the paper. The stories up until now were rather plain and boring, filled with interviews with background characters. It was a nice touch to keep all of us connected, but this morning that all changed. The starring headline declared, "Tottenstinker's Horrific Secret" and there was a picture of me holding the dead cat and looking dazed.

"What the-" I started scanning the article. According to it, Edwin and I had a huge fight at the restaurant and then I left, finding some poor stray in an alley and killed it. "This is all lies!"

"I know, but this is the only paper in the city. It's Author's voice in our everyday lives. We must do some damage control," Steven said. "I've already called for a press conference this morning."

"Let me finish getting ready and we'll go," I said. Steven helped me look my best and when I left I felt as powerful as I was meant to be. As the heroine, I should be able to clear my name quickly.

On the ride to the conference, Steven gave me pointers on what to expect. My driver offered to stand with me, having witnessed the whole thing. My memories let me know that this was not the first time this happened; the paper and I were at odds a lot.

The press conference was held in the front lobby of my office building. It was packed with reporters and protesters. I immediately spotted the brunette and blonde who accosted me on my first day. They were talking to a redhead woman.

"That's Lorna Bailey," Steven whispered. "The redhead. She's the reporter that put out that article. From what I've gotten from Author, she is some hotshot journalist who is city-wide famous for writing about the evils of your business."

"Yeah, I'm getting the same memories. Who are the people with her?"

"I don't have names for them yet, but I recognize them as the protesters from our first day."

"So do I. I was hoping you'd know more than me."

With that, I walked briskly up to the podium. As nervous as I was, I bet Author would help pull the right words out of my mouth. To my horror, I realized Author was nowhere to be felt. I was on my own in my first ever unauthorized scene.

"Thank you all for coming on such short notice," I said and the room slowly quieted. "I am sure you all saw this morning's article which maligned my good name. For such a great paper as the *City Times* has proven to be, I was shocked to see my name printed with such vicious lies and slander.

This tarrididdle will not stand and I demand that the *City Times* recants its story."

"So, you're saying you were not photographed holding a dead cat?" This came from Lorna in the back. I could see the smug smile on her face.

"Is a photograph always the truth? I noticed there was a lack of witnesses to my alleged crime, despite the streets being full at that time. Tell me, Lorna, was that because your accomplices did not wish for the fingers to be pointed at them?" At the sound of the other reporters gasping, I smiled. "You all heard it right! I was set up so that Lorna Bailey could invent falsehoods and sell more papers. In truth, there was no evidence beyond a photographed trap to this crime. Indeed," I held up my hands, "there is no evidence even on me."

"And what is that supposed to mean," snapped the brunette protester. I bit back my groan as I recognized Heather.

"Beside the fact your timetable doesn't match up, I am unscathed. I am a cat-fancier; I would never willingly or knowingly harm a cat. Even with that fact, I am sure no cat would go silently into that dark night. No, they would scratch and claw and bite for their lives. I am unscathed. Not a scratch on me. However, Lorna, I notice you and your friend there look like you've been in a battle."

Lorna and Heather both reached up and touched the scratches on their faces. I realized then that I felt no intrusion from Author last night, just as I felt nothing today. It disturbed me greatly to know that these two would go through such lengths unfettered by Author to discredit me. All the evils of my life had been under the direction of an Author, not on my own.

"You mentioned a time line," one reporter said as his partner took a picture of Lorna and Heather.

"Yes. I would not have the time to commit the crime. From the time I left the restaurant to the time the picture was taken was less than two minutes. Now, I do not know how long it takes to find and kill a cat, and I hope I never learn that, but I am sure it takes longer than two minutes. I was in full view of the public the whole time."

"You saying you never hurt cats is a lie," Lorna yelled. "What about your Cat Camp? You harm cats daily in your greed to create your devilish coffee."

"Ma'am, I am an ailurophile. It is fully against my nature to harm my cats," I said. I saw pens furiously scribbling my words down. "People, an ailurophile is a person who likes cats, as in a cat fancier. Please do not misinterpret my meaning."

"Ms. Tottenstinker is regularly visited by health inspectors to ensure that there is no harm to the cats. She passes each and every time," Steven said, stepping up to my side.

"Only because you pay them off," Heather snarled. Suddenly, I knew her name. It was Hannah. I had the eerie sensation that I knew her from my past.

"Ms. Tottenstinker will be entertaining the next round of inspectors soon. Why don't you come along to see how a typical inspection is performed?" Steven said. "Now, if all of you will join us in the conference room, we have set up a few tasting stations to sample the Tabby Pops Coffee best Winter sellers, before we take them off the market to make way for the new Spring flavors." Steven, like a pro, escorted the reporters to the next room. I breathed a sigh of relief and went to the office to work.

I spent my day on the phone with my Cat Camp manager. One of the cats had a cold, and another did not like the coffee beans she was fed.

"Well, let Nilla Krilla rest up. And take Dibble off the *Canephore* beans and start him on the *Arabica* beans. Maybe the caffeine is upsetting his stomach?" I told the manager. "The health of the cats comes first."

"Ms. Tottenstinker?" Steven poked his head into my office. "Your dress for tonight has arrived."

I quickly said my good-byes to my manager and motioned for Steven to enter. The dress was exquisite. Once upon a time, I was in a fairytale where the princess wore a dress with small diamond chips. Every movement caught the lights and caused her shine. This dress was a close second, where the black material sparkled under the lights with each step. There was a mask of a crescent moon to complete the look and a beautiful silk shawl.

"Oh, you will look so beautiful," Steven gushed. "Wait until Edwin gets a load of you in this. Girl, you are going to knock his socks off!"

"That's Mr. Van Der Woody III to you!" Edwin, dressed in a tux, walked briskly into my office, giving the gown a once over. With a slight sneer on his perfect lips, he said, "It's garish, don't you think?"

"I think it looks wonderful." Never had I been allowed to wear anything so wonderful. In nearly every Story I appeared, I wore out-of-date, hideous dresses that were designed to make me look horrible, or all black to show off the fact I was the villain.

Edwin sniffed. "You would like that thing. It's so...so..." He waved his hand around, trying to find the right word to describe my dress.

Hesitantly, I said, "Sensational? Wondrous? Marvelous?"

"No. The opposite of those things."

"Ostentatious?"

"Yes, that's it."

I looked back at my dress. "What don't you like about it, Edwin?"

"It's too much. Really, Verucca, it's too much frou-frou. This is a simple charity event." He rubbed the bridge of his nose. "It's my charity event. I know just what you are doing. It won't work. No one will really care about what you wear. They are there for the poor underprivileged platipi."

"Well, it's too late to change now," I said. "Give me a minute to get ready."

"A minute?"

"It's a figure of speech. I say a minute, we both know I mean at least half an hour."

Edwin rolled his eyes and waited in the hall. I quickly changed my clothes and pulled my hair back in a bun since I did not have a hair stylist to enchant me into a beautiful woman. I finished before my allotted half hour was up and went out to the hall to meet Edwin. He motioned for me to follow him and I ran to keep up.

In the elevator, I said, "You look nice."

"Of course I do."

"I don't know if you saw the news, but my day has not been the best," I said.

In a bored tone, Edwin said, "Yes, I saw the little conference you conducted. Really Verucca, can you try to not embarrass me tonight?"

"You have my word that I will do all I can to not

embarrass you."

We went out to his car, and it took my breath away. The entire car looked like it was dipped in silver, with black leather interior. "This is gorgeous," I said.

"It's a Bugatti Veyron. Ordinarily, by itself, it would be the most expensive car in the world, but this one is extra special." He patted the shiny silver body. "This is real white gold. The whole car is cast from pure white gold. And I have pure fourteen karat gold as details in the interior."

"Well, it's the most extravagant car I've ever seen."

The car drove smoothly, but there was a definite coldness between Edwin and I. Little details were starting to bother me. Would it be worth it to win him in the end? I had the feeling he truly did not like me.

# Chapter Five

His charity event was held at Ristorante Pui Rico de Te. The whole place overflowed with balloons and streamers and painted roses in crystal vases. Tables were pushed closer to the walls to open up the middle of the room for dancing and mingling. On the back wall was an electronic board, displaying the current count of monies raised. To my own delight, the numbers were still climbing. A cardboard cutout of a platypus in glasses sat next to the electronic board with a banner of "Glasses for Platipi" over him. All around me were the elite of Faycrest, dressed in the height of fashion. Each dress made mine look ordinary.

Even the catering staff was dressed up. Men and women both wore stylish tuxedos as they paraded around with silver platters filled with champagne and little hors d'oeuvres. All except one, and I found myself noticing her right away. A single blonde waitress wore what could only be described as the "sexy" version of the costume. While she did wear a jacket, she did not wear a real tux underneath. Instead, she wore what looked like a one-piece bathing suit with the top half made up to look like a ruffled dress shirt and the bottom was made of a sparkly material. Her long legs were encased in fishnet stockings and she wore the most impossibly high heels ever. Take off the jacket and stick rabbit ears on her, and she'd be ready to work in a gentleman's club.

There was something familiar about her, but I felt the weight of Author and couldn't think of where I knew her from. I was sure that was Author's doing. Trying to take my mind off of her, I made my way around the room. Edwin was already surrounded by his friends, and I decided to let him enjoy his time. I knew at some point he'd make the big announcement that we were engaged, and I wanted to remain near-by.

Taking a shrimp from a passing tray, I walked over to a group of people I recognized. Author allowed me to know that they were all business elites in the city.

"Edwin sure has outdone himself once again," one woman was saying. I felt a flush of pride that his charity looked to be a big hit. "He certainly knows how to throw a charity event."

A man answered her. "Yes, this event will be the talk of the city for years to come. Why, I do believe he's already surpassed his goal."

"This event is so much better than the last one. What was it for? Better school equipment for some podunk little town?" The woman chuckled. "I mean, who cares? Let's focus on the important things in life, like the poor platipi and their little eyes. Not what some no-name town needs."

"What else do you expect from Faycrest's resident crazy cat woman? Really, that Verucca can learn a thing or two from Edwin."

"What does he see in her? A man like him should be with a woman of equal beauty and grace. Not chained down with an old hag." The woman looked around the room, missing the fact I was standing not far behind her. She pointed out the blonde waitress. "There, see that woman. She would make a better match for Edwin than that Tottenstinker."

I cleared my throat and inserted myself into the little group. Somehow, I was not surprised to see that none of them were embarrassed that I overheard their conversation. With a smile, I said, "Enjoying yourselves?"

The woman gave a dissatisfied sniff. "I was. Seems ruined now."

"Oh, that's too bad," I said. "I'm sure Edwin would be sorry to hear you're not having fun. I know he tried so hard to make tonight extraordinary."

The man and the woman glared at me. We all knew that she was referring to me. I ruined the whole party for her. Well, tough. I have seen firsthand the kind of hurdles the heroine must leap over to achieve her happy ending. I could withstand a few snide comments.

At that moment, Edwin made his way to the middle of the room. The lights dimmed with only a bright light focused on him. The room immediately hushed.

"Thank you all for coming to my charity event," Edwin said. "I have two incredibly important announcements. For the first, if Verucca Tottenstinker can join me."

I knew what was coming. With butterflies in my stomach, I walked up to Edwin. He smiled at me, but it never reached his eyes. It was all for show.

"Everyone, as you know, Verucca and I have been dating for quite some time now. We are not getting any younger. On the first of the year, just as the clock struck twelve, I asked Verucca Tottenstinker to be my bride, and she said yes!"

The room fell in silence. I actually heard crickets chirping. Trying to laugh it off, I turned to Edwin, "I think they're holding their applause for your next announcement, dear."

"Oh, right. My final announcement is the tally of tonight's charity event. Thanks to all of you, we raised over seven million dollars for the poor, underprivileged platipi of the world. Give yourselves a hand, folks!"

This time, the room erupted with cheers and clapping. I applauded as well, stepping back to give Edwin the spotlight. He seemed to relish the recognition.

After that, I tried to make way around the room some more. A few people were glad to talk to me, congratulating me on the engagement and cooing over the ring. Mostly, though, people ignored me. This was fine by me. I was used to being ignored.

I was making my way back to Edwin when a sudden migraine struck me. I grabbed a table to keep from falling over as the pain pounded in my head. My vision blurred and I was worried I'd pass out. I straightened myself out and realized that I could not stay if I was in so much pain. I slowly made my way to Edwin, one hand against my throbbing temple while the other grasped at anything to keep me upright. Even with my blurred vision, I could see Edwin's disappointed face.

"Darling, I'm going to cut my evening short," I said once I was standing in front of him. "I fear I have a killer migraine."

Edwin sighed dramatically. "Can't it wait? It's too early to leave."

"I had a lovely time, Edwin, really I did. This migraine just hit me out of the blue."

"But you can't go." His voice wavered between whining and cold, as if he couldn't decide if he wanted me to stay or not. "Is it really tearing you up this much that my charity event is so successful that you want to leave?"

"What? No! Edwin -" I winced, rubbing my throbbing head. I felt sick and worried I'd embarrass myself. "I am thrilled for your success. Really I am. I love knowing that you've made a difference in the world. But, fact of the matter, I do have a migraine. I just need to go home."

"You expect me to leave my party early?"

It took me a while through the pain to fathom Edwin's words. Leave early? No, I was the one leaving early. What could he mean?

"I drove you here, Verucca. Remember? Or did you drink so much you've forgotten." His words were now cruel, bearing down on me.

"I plan on taking a cab," I said. "I forgot all about you driving, but I had no plans on making you leave."

Edwin snorted. "I'll bet. Verucca, you need to learn how to moderate yourself. You're falling down drunk. You promised to not embarrass me."

"I only drank water tonight, Edwin. I kept my promise." I moaned as the pain started to feel like knives stabbing my right eye. "I'll talk to you tomorrow."

"I suppose you want me to pay for your cab, or risk hearing you bitch about it in the morning," Edwin snapped.

"I'm capable of paying for my own cab. Good night, Edwin." I didn't bother waiting for his answer. I made my way out with as much dignity as I could. I was sure the pain made me look drunk, but I didn't bump into any one or fall over. I left the soiree with my head held high.

# Planning His Pleasure

Edwin frowned as he watched Verucca stumble drunkenly out of the restaurant. Her lies about not drinking and only merely having a headache were enough to give him gray hairs. This was supposed to be the woman he wanted to merge his business with, to spend his remaining years in perfect partnership. In truth, he knew he loathed the woman. She was as self-centered as they come. Imagine, leaving early because she had to share the spotlight. The nerve of some people! This was his shimmering moment and she had to go and ruin it.

He took a swig from his fluted crystal champagne glass. To top off his bad feeling, he just knew Verucca would make good on her threat to call him the next morning. Probably to complain about how awful the cab ride was or how disappointed she was in him not running out to soothe her poor soul. If only he could leave Verucca, but they both knew that was impossible.

"Um, excuse me, sir?" A sweet voice, as breathlessly airy as a fairy and as melodic as an angel, sounded from his left. Edwin turned to find himself face-to-face with the most beautiful woman he ever seen. Her heart-shaped face was framed by wavy golden hair, the most gorgeous blue eyes peered up at him through a curtain of perfect lashes, and the most kissable rosebud lips were tilted his way. She wore a sexy tuxedo costume that framed her curves perfectly and showed off her tiny waist. Long, luxurious legs were encased by the most sinfully erotic fishnet tights and ended in dainty high heels. Edwin's heart beat faster as he gazed at this vision of perfection, this Aphrodite sent down from the heavens to torment him.

He cleared his throat. "May I help you?"

The beautiful blonde smiled, stealing Edwin's breath away. "I overheard your, uh, fiancé mentioning that she had a headache. I took the liberty of getting her some aspirin and a coke."

"That's awfully kind of you. Far kinder than she deserves. But I doubt she really needed it. At least, not right now. When she wakes up with a hangover tomorrow, then she'll need it." Edwin exhaled heavily. "She just didn't want to be here."

"Oh, my, I can't imagine anyone not wanting to be here. This is going to be the talk of the city for years to come. Why, I've overheard several reporters talking about how much wonderful work you've done, sir. I'm sure you'll make the front page and every event ever in the city will be compared to this one." The angel gave a dreamy little sigh. "If I were a guest, I'd be so happy that I'd never want to leave."

This caught Edwin by surprise. "You're not a guest? I thought surely a woman as beautiful as you would be on the arm of any of the men here. And, please, call me Edwin."

"Oh, no. I'm just one of the catering staff." She gestured to her sexy outfit, which brought Edwin's eyes back to admiring her perfect curves. She clearly wasn't as stuffy or formal as the other caterers. She saw him looking at her and blushed. "It was a last minute choice. I'm helping out a friend and they didn't have a proper uniform for me."

"I think you look marvelous." Edwin took her hand and gently kissed the silken skin. At that moment, the band played a slow, romantic number. Inspired, he said, "Care to dance?"

"I really shouldn't. I'm supposed to be working, sir. They'll wonder what's become of me." The way she looked down, so modest, brought all of Edwin's fierce protectiveness to the front. He wanted to scoop her up and shower her with every treasure her heart desired. No one who looked like her should be working. She should be dancing.

"It's my charity ball," Edwin said. "If I wish to dance with the most beautiful woman in the room, I should have that right. If anyone bothers you, just let me know. From this moment on, you're my guest. And, please, I really insist you call me Edwin."

"I'm not the most beautiful woman in the room," she said humbly.

"I say you are. So, my Cinderella, may I have this dance? Or shall I wither away in the corner all night, dreaming of you?"

She giggled, a sound so blithesome that he felt the world was a better place because of it. "Cinderella? Me?"

"Why not? From caterer to star of the ball, sounds like Cinderella to me."

He led her out on the dance floor, marveling at how perfectly she fit in his arms. The band played only slow songs after that, allowing him more time to spend with this delicate Fey. She laid her head against his shoulder as they danced, their bodies moving in graceful circles.

"There is one problem about me being Cinderella," she whispered.

"Oh? What's that?"

"She marries the prince at the end."

Edwin smiled and tilted her face to his. "Who knows? Maybe you'll marry your prince in the end."

# Chapter Six

I awoke the next morning still feeling weak and as if my head were about to explode. The residue of the migraine lingered and every little noise magnified. The birds' aubade out my window sounded shrill, their joyous song greeting the dawn drilled holes in my aching skull. I rolled out of bed and managed to crawl to the shower. Normally, a good hot shower made me feel human. This time, I think I barely registered. Coffee, I decided, might help me along in becoming human.

After five minutes of searching the kitchen for my coffee machine, I admitted defeat and curled up in a comfortable chair by the fire place. For being the coffee queen, I did not own a coffee pot. I couldn't understand why I relied on Steven to bring me coffee in the morning.

Speaking of Steven, he was late. Nearly half an hour late, he came creeping into my apartment with his normal offerings of coffee and the morning paper. As silently as he could, he placed them on the table.

"I'm not asleep," I said.

"I know. It's just…don't shoot the messenger, okay? Today is not going to be a good day."

"Don't I know it? I feel awful." I slid out of the chair and slowly made my way to the table. Picking up the paper, the first thing I noticed was the date. "Wait, why are you coming over to bring me coffee and the paper on Sunday? For that matter, why on the weekends at all?"

"You don't rest, Verucca. You work the weekends. So must

I." Steven went into my kitchen. "Now, drink the coffee."

I took a sip and gave the paper a good reading. I nearly choked on my coffee at the first three stories that popped up. The top one was expected. Edwin's charity ball was the hit of the city, he made well over his intended goal, everyone had fun, and so forth. There was a nice picture of Edwin while he was making his announcement. So far, the news seemed okay.

The second story, however, made my stomach turn. There was a picture of me, slumped in the back seat of the taxi, with the headline, "Tottenstinker Drunk!" The article, written by Lorna of course, went on to talk about how I stumbled drunkenly from the party and got in a cab, of how I drank to excess due to my jealousy over Edwin's success, and how I just simply ruined the night of my fiancé with my ill-mannered behavior. I could feel the migraine returning.

"This is just a bunch of lies," I said. "I was not drunk! I suffered a migraine. I didn't even drink at the gala."

"Oh, honey, it gets worse," Steven said. "I'm going to hide the knives, if you don't mind. Keep reading and please don't throw the coffee on me."

"What could be worse than a bunch of lies?"

"A very nasty truth."

That was when the third headline jumped out at me. Steven was right, this one hurt even more than the lies printed above. There was another picture of Edwin, but he was dancing with that blonde caterer with the skimpy outfit. The story gave a glowing review of Edwin's romance with his mysterious Cinderella and how they danced the night away.

Almost mumbling to myself, I started to read the article. "A perfect fit, dear reader, which shows just how awful of a match our wonderful Edwin Van Der Woody III is with that hag Verucca Tottenstinker. Just look at how our Cinderella fits in his arms, how the room lights up around them. Yes, dear reader, they are the perfect couple." I put the paper down. "What a load of hooey! This prevaricator is a sorry excuse for a reporter. I doubt she'd know the facts or the truth if it bit her in the leg! She continues to malign me in print while she writes her panegyric fairytales of this perfect romance that will not be! There is no way I'm going to allow this little blonde upstart take away my story."

"You know," said Steven. "When you get angry, your vocabulary really blossoms. I have no idea half of what you said."

I had to think back on what I just said. "I believe I called the reporter a lying liar who writes lies about me while pandering and writing glowing reviews for little miss Cinderella."

"Ah, okay." Still standing at a distance, Steven said, "Um, maybe you're not the heroine? Maybe little miss Cinderella is?"

I threw the paper away. "But I'm not a villain. There is nothing evil about me. I don't need Edwin's money, so I'm not a gold digger. I'm not evil to my employees. I don't abuse anyone. There is nothing I can find that makes me the bad guy. This has to be my Story." I sighed. "This is just a bump in the road. I know it. In the end, Edwin will realize that character is more important than lovely looks and we'll have our riding off into the sunset."

"I hope you're right. I really do."

I finished my coffee, trying to calm down. I had to be right. This was my Story. Edwin was engaged to me. I personally didn't care what he did outside of the Story, but while we were here, he would pretend that he wanted to be with me. I went over in my head all the Stories I've engaged in, and how the heroine overcame any obstacle. It was obvious; I would be forever climbing over our Cinderella.

In truth, it didn't sit well with me that her nickname was Cinderella. That normally meant she would get the prince in the end. Well, I wasn't going to go down without a fight. How many times had I watched as my pretend marriages fell apart because Author made me the bad guy? How many times did I sit in the back of a church and watch as the golden pair get their happily ever after while I was doomed to end up alone? Not this time. Edwin was mine and I would get my ending.

As I watched Steven putter around the kitchen, I got to thinking about his Character. He was the Bob Cratchet to my Scrooge. I knew that I'd be lost without him. After all, he was coming in on the weekends to help me out when, by all rights, he should have a day off.

"So, Steven, I have to ask, is there anything you don't do for me? You come in here and bring me coffee every morning, you keep my schedule straight, and you seem to run all my errands. For as busy as I'm kept, I imagine you're ten times busier."

"Try twenty times and you might be close."

"I was thinking, you shouldn't have to run yourself ragged on my behalf. I want to promote you to my official right hand man and hire you an assistant. Granted, the job won't change, but now you'll have a larger salary and someone to delegate work."

"Sounds great to me. I can always use an extra pair of hands."

"Okay. I would like to get the interviews and such started

by next week, if possible." I picked up the planner Steven often carried around and flipped it open. "Let's see, I need to discuss the wedding budget with Edwin soon. Our meeting with Shirley Lovette is on Valentine's Day. That's only two weeks away and we're both so busy."

"And, don't forget you have a tour of the Cat Camp coming up." Steven took the planner. Frowning slightly, he said, "That looks like it was scheduled on the same day as Shirley."

"Neither can be rescheduled?"

"Nope. Shirley is booked solid and if we move the Cat Camp inspection, it'll look suspicious. I suppose we can try moving the Cat Camp inspection earlier." Steven frowned, tapping a pencil against the planner. "Problem there is that the important inspectors are often booked, and Author really wants it on the same day."

"Let it stand, then." I rubbed my temples, glad the last of the pain was finally fading. I felt like me again.

After I sent Steven home to enjoy his Sunday, I looked up the number for the newspaper. There was no way I'd let that story about me stand. The paper was not apologetic at all. Not even my threat to sue could make them change their tune.

"We have Author on our side. We print what she says to print," the man at the newspaper told me. "That means, we will always be right."

"What about justice and truth? The integrity of your paper is at stake. Print the truth, not just any old lie. I cannot fathom how you allow your paper to print when you don't investigate your stories."

"We did investigate. Or rather, Author investigated for us. Just because you got caught drunk doesn't give you the right to threaten us. Maybe you should stay away from alcohol!"

"I did! I had a migraine! There is a difference."

The next thing I heard was a click and then nothing. He hung up on me.

I called Edwin next. He did not sound pleased to hear from me. When he said he saw the paper, I hoped that meant he saw his story and would explain why he was dancing with another woman.

"You are a great embarrassment, Verucca," Edwin sneered. "Not only do you get drunk at my charity ball, but it makes the paper! People are talking! Do you have any idea how that makes me look?"

"Edwin, I only drank water last night. It was a migraine. We both know this. However, if you want to talk embarrassing, let's discuss the story in today's paper about you and your little blonde Cinderella? Do you know how embarrassing it is to me to know that the second I walk out of the room you're in the arms of another woman?"

"I was merely showing my guest a good time."

"She was part of the staff. You were under no obligation to show her a good time. And if that story is to be believed, you danced with her all night long. That's far above your duty as host, Edwin."

"I'm a good host, Verucca. Now, if you don't mind, those of us who are not hung over have work to do." With that, he hung up on me.

I spent the rest of the day curled up with my cat. My story was crumbling all around me. I could see my Happily-Ever-After fading before I could grasp it.

# Chapter Seven

The wedding planning office of Shirley Lovette, the Queen of Romantic Unions, was a visual nightmare. Zebra print as far as the eye could see nestled together with flashes of hot pink accents. Two of the walls were black and white striped, while the other two were so bright pink they made my eyes water. The chairs looked like she skinned a sparkly zebra wearing a boa. Even the receptionist, who ignored me when I walked in, wore the same color scheme.

Edwin was already there and looked uncomfortable. I wasn't sure if it was the decor or the fact that, for the past two weeks, stories about him and Cinderella were front page news. Everything from "innocent" little encounters in the park to full on dates at fancy restaurants. Whenever I brought the fact up, he told me I was blowing it all out of proportion.

"There you are, Verucca!" Edwin stalked over to me, pointing to his expensive watch. "Do you have any idea how long I've been waiting for you?"

I looked at my watch. "I'm five minutes early," I said. I shifted my bag on my shoulder, redistributing the weight of my wedding scrap book. I spent the past two weeks trying to get as much done on our wedding as I could. Edwin and I already discussed a budget and I ate lunch with my bridesmaids. I bought several books on how to plan a wedding and knew my timeline. I did all I could to make this easy on Shirley so we could get down to the hard part of planning a wedding faster.

"The meeting was rescheduled for an hour ago! You're

late, Verucca."

"I wasn't informed. When was this decision made?"

"This morning. We tried calling you, but you never picked up your phone."

I knew that was a lie. Neither mine nor Steven's phone rung all morning. I pulled my phone out to double check, and saw that it was, indeed, blank. Before I could comment on that, Author swooped in and we were ready to perform.

We sat in silence as the scene was set. I knew we didn't look like the happy couple we were supposed to be, but I was not going to give up on my Happily-Ever-After. Edwin was engaged to me, and we were going to fight the odds and have a wonderful wedding. There would be no rolling over for Cinderella. After all, only a villain would steal another woman's man.

Shirley came out to get us herself. Short and stout, she made up for her lack of height with her high beehive hairdo that was so bright red it screamed bottled. Her eyes were magnified by the cat's eye glasses she wore, the fake diamonds flashed under the lights. Her clothing matched the decor and clashed with her hair and she stank of cheap perfume. My first impression was 'not impressed'.

"So glad you could finally join us, Ms. Tottenstinker. Though, now all my appointments will be running late." Her voice held the raspy nature of one who smoked ten packs a day.

"I was busy at the office preparing for my afternoon meeting," I said. "My cell never rang." At least Author allowed me to tell the truth.

"I know we called you," Shirley said. "Check your phone." This time, several missed calls showed up.

"The reception must be bad," I said. "Why didn't you try calling my office directly?"

Shirley twittered as if I said something amusing. "We don't have that number, Ms. Tottenstinker."

I knew that was a lie. I lived at my office. There was no way I would not have given them that number. In fact, I had a clear memory of doing so.

Shirley escorted us from the horrendous waiting room to an equally ugly office. Waiting for us was a familiar blonde in a soft pink dress, so short that the skirt of it practically disappeared as she crossed her legs. The blonde protester, our mysterious Cinderella. Author forced me to keep my silence, pressing into me that I didn't recognize her.

"Everyone, this is my assistant, Sophie Winslow." Shirley beamed, patting Sophie on the shoulder. "Dare I say, she's my heir? She comes up with the most wonderful ideas for weddings and she's the most helpful person I know."

Edwin smiled and straightened his tie. "What kind of helpful things are you in to, Sophie?"

I wanted to roll my eyes. His acting as if he never met her was so obvious. She giggled and blushed and he ducked his head like a shy school boy, stealing glances of her every now and again. I cleared my throat to remind them I was still in the room.

"I mostly help my friend with her animal protection group," Sophie said. Her voice was even more ethereal than before, the light, airy tone making her sound not all there. "I just love animals. I can't stand it when people harm them." She shot a glance at me.

"That is so noble of you," gushed Edwin. He sat right next to her, his attention all on her.

I took the seat farthest from Sophie. "I did some research," I said. "Edwin and I agreed to a wedding at the end of the year, around the Christmas holidays. We have our budget set up," I pulled the worksheet out of my scrap book and handed it to Shirley, "and I've pulled the designs of a few wedding ideas that caught my eye. I'm actually partial to an outdoor wedding; something by the beach would be nice."

"The beach would be too cold in December," Edwin said.

"We can travel." I pulled out the page on beach weddings. "If we do the wedding at a resort, we can have the ceremony out on the beach and the reception inside. It might not be as big as other weddings, but I think a smaller, more intimate affair would be best."

"You think, you think, you think," Edwin said. "None of that is what I think."

Shirley frowned. "Destination weddings are the worst. Your guests don't want to travel during the holidays."

"It doesn't have to be far. I'm sure we can find a venue close to home. Maybe a lake or something?"

"No!" Shirley slammed her hand down on her desk. "People do not wish to travel to a wedding. It's just not done! They want a wedding close-by and inside. They do not want to drive to a beach for a wedding in the middle of winter."

"You arranged my friend Bambi's wedding in Hawaii at the top of a volcano. Are you telling me that it's more plausible for people to fly several hours to a wedding than it is for them to possibly drive two hours?"

"Yes."

"I have to agree with Shirley," Edwin said. "Who wants to get married at the beach? The sand would get into everything and the whole place reeks of dried seaweed. Not to mention the bugs in the food."

"Oh, and it would look cheap," Sophie added. "Beach weddings are only done by the destitute who can't afford a good wedding. You don't want anyone to say you're cheap, do you Ms. Tottenstinker?"

"And so clichéd," Shirley cut in. "And I would hate to think of what that sea air and sand would do to your wedding gown. No, it's better to not have a beach wedding."

I bit my tongue. Several celebrities wedded beach-side and made it sophisticated. Cheap was not the word I'd use for their weddings.

"Maybe we can rent out a nice house or hotel near the beach for everyone to stay," I suggested.

"No." Shirley's tone indicated that matter was closed.

I sighed, shifting through my file. "Okay, so something closer to home. We have some lovely wineries just outside the city. Many of them have their own restaurants and wedding venues, and the scenery would be gorgeous. Why not try there?" I pulled out several brochures I printed. "Let's see, we have The Night Grape Winery, Sapphire Springs, and The Merry Turtle; all of which have a wedding venue. And there's Dainty Grape and Gambrinus wineries; both of which just have a personal restaurant and are located overlooking Faycrest. The night views would be marvelous. And, if the weather is going to be bad, we can always relocate inside the winery."

All three of them looked aghast. One would have thought I suggested holding our wedding on top of a garbage pile.

"Have you gone mad? What makes you think I'd have my wedding at any of those places," Edwin demanded. "They are my rivals! If we were even to consider holding our wedding at a winery, it would be at my very own Dancing Ladies Winery."

I had not known he owned a winery. "So, I should add your winery to the list?"

"No! We will not have the wedding there. The very thought!" Edwin slumped in his chair, folding his arms and looking like a petulant child.

"Not to mention having it a winery promotes drinking," Shirley said. "Your guests can get too drunk and break more than you can pay for. Or drive drunk! Oh, Ms. Tottenstinker, how dare you suggest that your guests drive drunk!"

"The weather will still be a problem," Sophie said. "And it's in winter! It won't be as pretty in winter. Or around Christmas time. No one wants to attend a wedding around Christmas time. They'd rather be home with their families." Sophie shuddered. "Plus, they would probably all be wearing ugly Christmas sweaters. You don't want that."

"We can hold it before or after Christmas," I said. I didn't bother bringing out the Christmas-themed ideas I collected.

"So far, Verucca," Edwin said, "you have come up with cheap and horrible ideas. I don't think you are cut out for this." He turned to Sophie. "You're the expert. What kind of wedding would you suggest?"

Sophie smiled, twirling a lock of her blonde hair around one slender little finger. "I'm a bit of a traditionalist," she said. "My ideal wedding would be at the cathedral in the center of the city. It looks just like a castle, and I always wanted a fairytale wedding." She sighed. "I can just picture it; there I am in a dress befitting a princess, walking down an aisle decorated with an abundance of flowers toward my prince. I'd have rows of bridesmaids dressed in pink and cream, and the groomsmen to match. We'd leave in a carriage to go dine at one of the upscale restaurants and everything would just be magical."

"As pretty as that sounds, I do not want a fairytale wedding," I said. "I want something that looks sophisticated, with a location outside of a church." I pulled out a few more ideas. "I want a wedding that is fun for everyone. Maybe a Christmas color scheme since it's close to the holidays. We can find a venue that is not a cathedral that will accommodate our guests."

"No, I like Sophie's idea. What little girl doesn't want to be a princess," Edwin said, his eyes on Sophie.

"Edwin, picture me coming down the aisle, if you will," I said. "Since this wedding is coming out of my bank account, I should have the final word. And my word is no to a church wedding."

"Sophie's idea is the best," Shirley said. "Everyone loves a church wedding. It's local and simple, yet elegant. Your guests won't have to travel. It'll be indoors. Yes, it's perfect!"

"I have no religious affiliation," I said. "Why would I want a wedding in a building in which I don't subscribe to that faith?"

"Then it shouldn't bother you," Edwin said. "It's just a building after all."

"That's not my point!"

"Really, Verucca, why are you being so stubborn? It's just a building."

"I'm the one paying for this, Edwin. I do not want the whole church wedding. If we must have an indoor wedding, then I want it at a venue." I pushed over a small stack of papers I gathered. "Look, we have several places in the city where we can get married. The Estate Bed and Breakfast is big enough and grand enough for a wedding, or the Mayor's Manor Hotel. Our guests can stay there; it has a ballroom for the ceremony, an indoor garden for cocktail hour while the ballroom is rearranged for the reception. We can even get married at the catacombs under the city. They have a wedding in their brochure, Edwin."

Edwin barely looked at the pages before handing them to Shirley, who threw them away. "The cathedral will work out just fine, Verucca," he said. "Besides, who wants to get married in the catacombs? That's so...Gothic."

Sophie stifled a giggle. "I do think Gothic describes Ms. Tottenstinker."

"So, that's settled," said Shirley. She typed the note on her computer. "Wedding held at the cathedral in later half of December. Now, what colors are we having?"

"Red, green, and gold," I said. "Christmas colors."

"Pink and cream and gold," said Sophie. "They are much better for a fairytale wedding."

"My wedding is not a fairytale," I said.

"More like a nightmare," muttered Edwin.

"Christmas colors are so tacky," Sophie said. "Everyone would expect that."

"Sophie's right," said Shirley. She made another note, and then looked at me. "Well, at least you'll be wearing cream to the wedding. I don't think pink would be your color."

"This is not how a wedding planner works," I said. "It's my wedding."

Shirley scoffed. "Oh, so now you're an expert? I happen to be the foremost wedding planner in the entire city. I know what's best, not you."

"I'm sure there are other wedding planners, or I can do this all on my own. I do not want a pink wedding at a church. I am not a pink person, nor am I a church person."

"Quit being so rude, Verucca," snapped Edwin. "They are the experts. Just, for once, will you let someone else do their job without you acting like you know best? You obviously don't know the first thing about planning a wedding. Sophie does, so let her do her job."

Before I could say anything, my phone rang. I picked it up, hearing Edwin mutter about how rude I was being, and saw that I got a text from Steven. 'Car out front'

"I need to go. I have another meeting today." I turned to Edwin. "Do not sign anything without me. None of this will be valid without my signature anyway, but I do not want you getting us into a contract that doesn't suit my needs. For the record, no pink church wedding. At all!"

I left, turning back once to see Edwin and Sophie with their heads together, planning a wedding. They looked like the engaged couple. This did not bode well.

# Chapter Eight

My private car drove Steven and me to the Cat Camp at the other end of Faycrest. Along the way, I got a chance to see the Cathedral, located in the middle of the city with two huge gardens filled with various religious statues. While it was big and elegant-looking, it was not what I wanted. Having spent all of my Stories as the wicked stepmother or cold-hearted orphanage director, I saw my fair share of church weddings. They were all appealing, but it made me want something special if I were to ever get the chance to wed. Especially a pink wedding! Every single downtrodden Cinderella or hopelessly abused heroine I ever witnessed had a pink wedding.

"Could Author be any more obvious?" asked Steven when I told him how the meeting with Shirley had gone. "Anyone who knows anything about wedding planners will know that the scene was wrong. Author will get letters from angry fans."

"I guess this is a Cinderella Story with a twist," I said. "I mean, Sophie isn't exactly the poor and harassed worker who needs a prince to sweep her off her feet. She has a good job and is set up for a promotion. From what I could see, she's not exactly poor or starving. If this were any other Story, I'd think her showing up would portend a shift in my fortunes for the worse. In every Story I've participated in, the motif would show me as the evil antagonist, and I would know it. I am too much of a good person to be the antagonist. I mean, when I first met Sophie, she poured red paint on me. And her friends killed a cat. How are those the actions of the protagonist?"

Steven shrugged. "I hope you're right, Verucca. I did some digging in your background, and I'm having a hard time picturing you as a bad guy. Did you know you give to charities on a regular basis? Not silly charities like glasses for platipi, but real, honest charities. Like band equipment for underprivileged schools and blankets for the homeless."

"Yeah, that's what I'm talking about. I do not have the background of the evil stepmother or stepsister to complete this Story. There must be something we're missing."

Cat Camp sat nestled on over ten acres of farmland. There was a single two-story building, roughly 25,000 sqft, sitting in the middle of the property. It was painted to look like a barn, but no barn was ever that big. Chain-link fences sectioned off various areas of the land with cat toys all over the place. In some of the sections, I could see my employees watching as the cats frolicked merrily on the many cat towers or chased jingle balls and catnip mice.

As the Cat Camp came into view, we saw the assembly waiting for us. There seemed to be three distinctive groups; the inspectors in their professional suits and clipboards, the reporters with camera crews, and a small gathering of protesters, waving signs that proclaimed my cruelty to animals. At the moment, the reporters mingled with the protesters, filming their antics, but once they realized I was approaching, they turned the cameras in my direction.

"I didn't think so many would show up," I said.

"I know none of them sent word they'd be here," Steven said. "Ready for the circus?"

"As ready as I'll ever be." The car pulled up to the edge of the crowd. The reporters pushed close on one side, ready to shove a camera or microphone in my face when I exited. The protesters took the other side, forming a gantlet for me to walk through. I tried to see if anyone carried a bucket, but I could not see if there were any present.

Taking a deep breath, I exited the car. The sea of bodies pressed close as the reporters asked how I felt about the protesters, and the protesters declaring I would burn in Hell. I held my head high and ignored both groups. Instead, I headed right to the inspectors. I knew each of them, the Story letting me know that I worked with them on several occasions.

"Welcome to the Tabby Pops Cat Camp," I said, shaking their hands. "I am so glad you've taken time out of your busy day to come and view my little clowder of lucky cats. I am sure it will all meet your approval."

"Did she just say she puts the cats in a chowder," a voice shrieked. I turned to see a familiar dark-haired woman: Heather.

"I said clowder. It means a group or cluster of cats." I turned back to the inspectors. "Shall we begin, gentlemen? I am sure you have more important things to do today."

I started the tour in the lobby. For the reporters' sakes, I gave a brief overview of my work. Much of the information only came to me moments before I spoke, and rather took me by surprise. I built Tabby Pops from the ground up by experimenting with my own cats before I owned my company. I got the idea in high school and spent my college years studying business and figuring out how to mass produce cat coffee on a cheaper scale than the civet cat coffee, the inspiration for my own business. I borrowed the money to start Tabby Pops as a small shop, and made enough to pay the money back before the year was up. I went from nothing to having a multi-million dollar industry.

"I now have over two hundred cats in about four different breeds. We rotate them around so that no cat is expected to work all year. Their diets and health are vital, and we have spa days for our cats. In those days, they are given a special bath and little massage. A happy cat will produce more than one who is uncomfortable. All of the cats are watched over by a team of no less than two assistants and one vet." I led them through the doors into the main portion of the Cat Camp. "This is the sleeping room for our working cats. Just outside those doors on the far end is an inside play area for days like today, when it's too cold to go outside. As you saw driving in, we do have an outside play area. The cats can climb and scratch to their little hearts content, or play with little toy mice and birds."

There were ten cages in the room, each one at least five feet by five feet with a large cushion, personal litter box, food and water bowls and a small box of toys. The cats had enough room to not feel boxed in, and several cats were being petted by the assistants. Despite having so many cats in one room, it did not smell like a litter box. Huge overhead fans helped circulate air and I knew the litter boxes were changed on a daily basis.

Behind me, I heard Lorna sneer, "I knew they had cages."

"I bet the cats are terrified," Heather said. "She probably beats them daily."

"If you wish to inspect the cats, please do so," I said, indicating the inspectors. "Now, this is just one room for our working cats. We have five more rooms set up, along with a cat spa." They moved around the room, looking over each cat. Each one passed as happy and healthy. The only incident we encountered was when Heather snatched one cat away from the assistant holding it, and the cat scratched her.

"See! They are not happy," Heather cried.

"Ma'am, Bobbles does not like to be grabbed," the assistant said. "He has to get used to you before you can hold him. He saw you as a threat."

Bobbles, a cute gray cat with a patch of black fur on his chin, came up to me. He wrapped himself around my legs and purred until I picked him up. Like a spoiled cat, he settled himself boneless in my arms and his purring increased in volume. If I didn't know better, I'd swear he was making a point to Heather.

"I just don't get this whole cat poop coffee thing," sneered Lorna. "How can you justify it?"

"The process used to make our coffee is just like the civet cats, who make *Kopi Luwack*, our cats are fed the coffee beans fresh off the branch. In their digestive tract, the beans transform and come out flavored. We triple wash the beans before roasting them, but they still hold the unique flavor brought on by the cat's digestive system. In order to make our special flavored beans, the beans are roasted in a special mixture. Not to fear, we don't feed our cats anything that can harm them. I have a fully-staffed veterinary office on site that works twenty-four hours a day, ready for any cat emergency."

"Well, it all looks in order, Ms. Tottenstinker," said one the inspectors. "Just like all the times we've come out. I've never seen happier cats in my life." He gave a deep laugh. "This job I want in my next life. Just sit around and be pampered."

"Thank you," I said. "If everyone will follow me, we have set up a sampling station in the lobby. If you've ever wanted to try Tabby Pops Coffee, now is the chance. I am aware that the price may not be economically sound for everyone to just enjoy. We are offering our dark roast and a chance to try our upcoming Spring flavor, Hawaiian Dreams. It's a blend of our vanilla light roast, mixed with Hawaiian grown macadamia nuts, coconuts, and just a dash of chocolate."

Heather gave a gasp. "Chocolate is poison to cats and you're feeding them all of this!"

"No, we only feed them the coffee beans. The rest of the ingredients are added at time of roasting," Steven said. "Please follow me."

As the group followed Steven to the lobby, I made a note to beef up my security. I did not like the idea of having Heather anywhere near my cats. It was bad enough that I was almost positive that Lorna would spin some yarn about me abusing my cats, but I had a feeling Heather was the kind of person who would steal them. Once everyone left, I pulled Steven aside.

"I want security doubled until further notice."

"I agree. I would have done that anyway. I overheard that Lorna and her friend talking about the cats needed to be rescued and Lorna photographing Heather's scratches."

I sighed, picking up the dirty cups. "If it weren't so early in the story, I'd feel as if I were near the twist."

"What twist?"

"The False Victory. You know, like in *Cinderella* where the evil stepmother locks her in the room the night of the ball, or in *Red Riding Hood* where the wolf gets to Grandma's house first. The part where the villains seems to have won just moments before they are defeated. If this happened further down the road, and if I were the villain, I'd say this was it. I look like I won, my business is sound and my practices legit, and then the real heroine pulls the rug out from under me with some Deus Ex Machina."

"Or, it could be one more setback for you. How many times does Cinderella think she's about to fail before she wins," Steven asked.

"True."

We cleaned the lobby before leaving. Steven's car was magically parked out front and my driver took me home. When I got there, I saw that I missed a call from Edwin. Smiling, I quickly called him back and was horrified to find out he signed a contract with Shirley for a pink and cream fairytale wedding at the Cathedral. Not only that, but he wanted Sophie to be our personal planner.

"She has such great ideas," Edwin gushed. "You should have seen the pictures she was showing me for how the bridesmaids' dresses could look. Not to mention her idea for a cake. It's just wonderful, Verucca."

"Well, as wonderful as you think it is, it's not legal. I never signed anything, and I need to be on the contract for them to plan our wedding."

"Not a problem. I forged your name. I knew you'd agree anyway."

"Edwin, that's ille-"

"Oh, and we're going to go with Sophie to audition restaurants. For a fairytale wedding, we need to eat at only the most elegant and swanky restaurant. Our guests will be talking about this for years."

"But signing my name is ille-"

"Just leave the planning to Sophie. Good lord, Verucca, we both know how horribly you plan anything. Your last charity event didn't even make the paper. I have much better planning skills and Sophie…" He sighed happily. "…She has the most amazing ideas." He hung up on me before I could protest.

No, this did not bode well for me at all.

# Chapter Nine

Things were tense for the next two weeks as February slowly warmed into March. There were three attempted break-ins to the Cat Camp, one act of vandalism that resulted in over five hundred dollars in damages, and several whispered threats to my staff. The police refused to do anything, stating that it was Author's will. My wedding plans continued to become The Sophie Show. When, a week after meeting with Shirley, Edwin and I got our engagement pictures taken, I was forced to wear a pink sundress that was ill-fitted for me. It was no surprise to learn it fit Sophie exactly.

The pictures were a disaster. My skin came out looking a sickly yellow and Edwin never smiled. I rejected every picture, but Sophie had the last word and the newspaper printed the one picture of me looking like an evil witch. When I got the bill from the photographer, I noticed it was twice as much as he quoted.

"Oh, we did some extra photos," he explained.

"What extra photos?"

"Of Edwin and that nice Sophie. They make such a perfect couple. It is really a shame the paper couldn't print one of their pictures instead."

Sophie continued to worm her way into all of my plans. Today was no exception. A bride should feel excited to go shopping for her wedding dress, but I had Sophie to worry about. Thankfully, she was busy and would not be joining me. Instead, she left a five page, detailed note with Steven telling me exactly what I should shop for, where I should shop, and let me know that my bridesmaids would be going with me. Sophie gave them their own lists, so I could not cheat and get something not Sophie-approved.

"I don't know who she thinks she is," I huffed. I stalked around my kitchen while Steven sipped my morning coffee with Diamond on his lap. "I can pick out my own dress! Have you seen her style? I will not look good in anything she deems Chic. Gah! Can you picture me in some princess pink ball gown monstrosity with sparkles?"

"Nope. You are more of a classic lines lady. Now, white might not be your color, but I bet you'd look great in a cream or even a colored dress."

"This is going to be a disaster. I can feel it." I slumped down in the seat next to him. "Steven, I'm starting to think that this isn't my Story after all. None of the other heroines I've ever interacted with went through this much. I mean, yeah, I made life hard on them, but they had armies of people who helped them out. It's not that I'm not grateful for you, but you're my only ally. My God! Rapunzel had more support than me, and she was locked in a tower her whole Story."

Steven snorted. "You're just making that one up. I've read the original Story, and she had no help."

"You know what I mean. I don't even feel like Author is on my side."

Steven watched me for a moment. "Have you given up on the Happily Ever After?"

I sighed, pushing myself back out of my seat and resumed my pacing. "A Happily Ever After with Edwin; yes. But not on the whole concept all together. I really don't see Edwin and myself entering that perfect halcyon ending where we ride off into the sunset in wedded bliss."

"What about an ending where you dump him and live as a strong, independent woman who don't need no man."

"That could be an option if Author hasn't beaten us over the head with how perfect a match Sophie and Edwin are." I slumped back down and laid my head on the table. "I really just want to back off and let them have their perfect wedding, but Author isn't allowing that either."

Steven rubbed my back. "Hang in there. I'm sure things will get better. After all, you have a pure heart, Verucca. People like you deserve the happy ending."

Soon, far too soon, it was time to meet my bridesmaids to go dress shopping. I took the list left by Sophie and had my driver take me to the meeting spot. My first store was a trendy wedding shop called Wedding Belles. The windows out front all featured various exquisite wedding dresses. Each one was fashionable with lace and satin and just the right amount of glitter. When walking in, I saw a dress boasting to have real diamonds and another one that was practically a lingerie bodice top with a flowing waterfall of taffeta. Maybe I misjudged Sophie. This was not what I expected. I ran my fingers over a beautiful satin mermaid-style wedding gown, picturing what I'd look like in such a dress.

"Verucca! There you are!" Standing around one particularly lovely dress were my bridesmaids. They were all tall and slender, wearing skimpy outfits and a ton of jewelry. Bambi Dixhorn, my friend with the wedding on the volcano, was a blonde woman with an obvious fake tan and bright pink painted bee-sting lips. Amanda Reckonwith was her twin with brown hair and red lips. Virginia Slims had red hair and wore the only pantsuit in the lot. Rosie Lydale and Latona Davenport were both Black; Rosie the slender one with gold streaks in her hair and gold make-up, and Latona the pleasantly plump one in zebra print and scarily long fingernails. They were all trophy wives of successful men in the city.

"Ladies," I greeted, "are we ready to shop?"

"They have the most beautiful dresses here," Bambi gushed. "I knew this would be wonderful when I heard you hired Shirley as your planner. Oh, that Sophie is just amazing. She planned out my whole wedding, and you know how fabulous that was."

I gave a small, tight smile. "She is something else," I said.

One of the store assistants brought me to a back room. She announced she already pulled a few dresses based on Sophie's recommendations. I agreed to try those on, but I saw a few dresses out front I'd like to try as well. Soon the dresses came in, and I was not thrilled with Sophie's choice. Each one was "vintage" in a way that looked like they were made from grandma's doily collection. The thick lace dresses were frumpy and did not look good on me. True to my word, I showed them to my bridesmaids.

"Oh, that one is just classic," Virginia breathed as I stepped out in the third option. It was a long-sleeved dress with thick lace from the neck to hem, and it itched. The lace was actually turning yellow.

"This really isn't me," I said.

The sales associate sniffed. "Miss Sophie's directions were to put you in something vintage. She knows best."

"Then how about something vintage inspired?" I pointed to a dress to my right; a beautiful long-sleeved silk gown with classical lines and a lace train.

"No. We will go with what Sophie suggested."

"Verucca, don't fight her," Bambi said. "Sophie knows all about weddings. If she thinks you'll look best in a real vintage dress, just go with it."

"I don't like these dresses. Shouldn't a bride feel beautiful in her dress? I should look in the mirror and be wowed by what I see. Not feel like I am playing dress up with a gown made from doilies."

Amanda rolled her eyes. "You just want to be in charge. You need to give up the control to Sophie. She's the wedding expert. We follow your advice on coffee, so you should follow her advice on weddings."

"I don't think I'm going to find what I want here," I said. "Let's try the next shop."

The girls grumbled about how we were going to be early, but I didn't care. The next shop was even more high-class. I could see other groups being served champagne and the dresses here were even more beautiful. This place would not have anything in the grandma vintage section.

"Excuse me, are you Verucca Tottenstinker?" A woman in a suit came up and her name tag stated she was the manager.

"Yes. I know I'm a little early. I can look around until my appointment time," I said. I was already eyeing a wonderful gown with a subtle touch of diamonds on the bodice. That would be perfect for me.

"No, ma'am. You will find nothing here."

I blinked. "Sorry? What?"

"None of my dresses are for you. Nothing I have will look good on you. I am disappointed that someone as wonderful as Sophie would send a creature like you to me. Go away. Maybe you can find a dress at some trinket shop?"

"You have hundreds of dresses," I said. "What do you

mean you have nothing that would look good on me?"

The manager frowned. "Ma'am, my dresses are for real women."

"I am a real woman."

"No. You are ugly. My dresses bring out the beauty of women, and you have no beauty. I have nothing for you. Go on. Shoo!"

"She does have a point," Latona said. "One can only dress up ugly so much before they have to admit it's ugly."

Embarrassed, I left the store. I knew Steven tried to warn me that this wasn't my Story, but I kept my head in the sand. This shopping trip was the incunabula of my journey to realization that I was not the heroine. The more stores we went to, the more I was rebuffed. I was too ugly, too flat, or too 'un-womanly' for any dresses that were not the most hideous in the store. I spent the ride home crying as I was forced to admit that I was the villain. Sophie was the virtuous heroine, her word was law. My halcyon belief shattered around me.

"Really, Verucca, all these tears for nothing," Bambi said. "You should go back to the first shop and get one of the dresses you tried on. Those were just right for you."

"Yes, Verucca. Quit being a drama queen," Virginia said.

"This hasn't been fun for us, either," said Amanda. "You drag us to all these stores and then leave in a huff when you're told the truth. Really, what did you expect? Do you not own a mirror? Surely you knew you were no beauty queen."

"I expect equality! I expect to be treated like any other client there to spend money. I expect them to show me dresses that I like and not tell me to leave because I am not their ideal of beauty!"

"Ma'am?" The driver knocked on the divider. "There is one more shop in town. It's on the way home. Would you like to try there?"

"There are no more stops," said Latona. "We went to every high-end store."

"This one isn't as high-end," the driver said. "Ma'am, it's your call."

As much as I didn't want to be embarrassed again, I knew there were no other shops on the list. Wherever this store came from, it was not one of Sophie's choices. That little bit of logic brought me some comfort.

"Yes, let's try it. Leave no stone unturned."

The store was a tiny shop tucked away in a strip mall. It was not the fancy dress store that Sophie wanted me to go to, and they did not have my name on the books for an appointment. However, I saw the perfect gown on entering. Not only were the lines classic, but it was a winter dress. That was something Sophie forgot when ordering my dresses. My wedding was in the winter, and the dress should reflect that.

As I walked around the gown, I knew it was the one. The off-the-shoulder fur cuff and fur cuffs on the sleeves were a slight cream color and the long-sleeved silk gown was a light pink. The skirt bunched slightly on one side, held up by a pink and gold pin that added just the right bit of sparkle to this outfit.

"This is the dress," I said.

"Oh, we can't let you try that one on," said the sales associate as she came over.

"Why not?"

"It's sold." She pulled out the tag to show me the sale.

"You don't have anything else like it?"

The sales associate bit her lip as she thought. "Well, yes. But not in these colors. It's red and black, not appropriate for a wedding."

"Let me try it on anyway. The colors don't matter. It's the style of the dress I'm more interested in."

The sales associate sighed and brought out the dress. Though I was supposed to look for a pink and cream dress, the black and red version looked marvelous on me. The red fur seemed to pop next to my pale skin and the dark black silk dress. The pin on the side sparkled even more merrily against the dark colors.

"Oh, I like this," I breathed. "It's perfect."

"It's ugly," said Bambi.

"You look like a witch," said Rosie.

"Edwin won't like it," Amanda pointed out.

"Don't care," I said, modeling the dress. Yes, at all angles, it looked good. "He planned my whole wedding without me, so why shouldn't I get a dress that I like?"

Virginia turned to Latona. "See, she's such a drama queen."

"Don't care," I repeated. I turned to the sales associate. "As much as I love this version, how soon can you order it in the pink and cream? The wedding isn't until December, but I'd like to have the dress early in case we need any alterations."

"The pink and cream is a one-of-a-kind. You can't order it."

"Are you sure," I asked. "My wedding colors are pink and cream." I detested Sophie's color choices, but in an effort to achieve some peace, I was honestly trying to find a dress that matched her theme. I glanced once more at the mirror and wished for a wedding of my choosing.

"Ma'am, the pink and gold version was made especially for a client. The only version of that gown for sale is the one you have on, and as I said, it is not befitting a bride."

"Verucca, just go with the first dress you put on," Bambi pleaded. "You can't wear black! It would ruin everything!"

"If I can't get this in pink and cream, then I will get it in the black and red. The wedding is months off, the color scheme can be changed. I will not be cowed into submission to wear an ugly dress. This is perfect for me, and this is the dress I will wear."

My mind was made up. I could change the color scheme for my wedding to something elegant that fitted the gown. I wanted this dress more than I ever wanted anything of material worth before.

I purchased the dress and made an appointment to have alterations done in six months. I knew Author was watching, but this was not a scene. I didn't know what she would make of this, and in that moment, I didn't care.

That night, I got a call from Edwin. Someone told him about my shopping trip, and he was furious. Sophie cried in the background about how I was ruining everything, and Edwin became her white knight.

"How can you buy a black dress? Do you have any idea what that would look like?"

"I'm well aware. However, as we are in the early planning stages, we can change the wedding colors," I said. "Black weddings are exceptionally chic."

"Not on the bride! Only depraved Goths wear black dresses!"

"If you don't want me to wear the black one, I suggest finding the same dress in pink and cream," I said. "That is the only dress I will wear."

"Sophie did a lot of work to find dresses for you to try on. What is so wrong with those dresses, Verucca? God, can't you just put your self-importance on a shelf long enough to let an expert help you?"

"It's this dress or I walk down the aisle naked. Your choice."

"I knew better than to trust you to do this," Edwin snapped. "Sophie will get you a dress and that's what you'll wear!"

"Like Hell! I'm paying for this wedding, and I will have some say in it. The dress stays! Black and red or pink and cream, it matters not." I slammed the phone down. I was the villain, and I would fight this heroine to the bitter end. Sophie will have her Happily Ever After over my dead body.

# Chapter Ten

Edwin did not speak to me again for two weeks. This made our engagement party awkward. Through the whole fancy bacchanalia, Edwin spent his time at Sophie's side, who sobbed that I ruined *her* wedding. The black wedding dress was going to stick out at the wedding since Sophie was unwilling to change the color scheme. None of my protests that it was *my* wedding that *I* was paying, or that a black wedding could be chic could sway her. In the end, I issued a challenge to Sophie.

"If you can find the exact same dress in pink and cream - for I know it exists - I will wear that instead. Every bride deserves to feel beautiful at her wedding, and this dress made me feel beautiful. If you can't find it, then we will change the color scheme to black and red."

Sophie sniffed and hid her face against Edwin's side. She mumbled, "You should have just bought one of the dresses I set aside for you. They would have suited you much better."

"I am not kidding when I say it's this dress or I walk down the aisle naked. Those are my terms, Sophie. I will wear that dress, either in black or in pink, or I will wear nothing at all."

Sophie agreed to find the dress, but spent the rest of my party in a corner. All of my guests made it a point to tell me how cruel I was being to her. I did not care. Had this been any other Story, I would have been in the right

In early March, we started looking for our perfect reception hall. Sophie had not come up with my dream dress in her colors, and Edwin never let me forget that. I told him she had only until June to find the dress. After that, it would take a miracle to get the dress in on time. All things considered, I was being exceedingly fair.

The first restaurant we went to "audition" was, of course, the most expensive and trendy restaurant in the entire city. It made Ristorante Piu Ricco di Te look positively shabby. This place was Sophie's suggestion and, much to my annoyance, she had to tag along.

"I really think we can decide if we like a restaurant without Sophie's help," I said as we waited outside for Sophie to arrive.

"Verucca, don't be so rude," Edwin snapped. "One would think you could go dress shopping alone, but we both know you failed on that. Sophie has gone above and beyond for our wedding and this is just a nice way to say thank you."

I snorted. We both knew why Sophie was going "above and beyond" her duty, and it had nothing to do with wanting our wedding to be a success. No, she was planning her wedding. I could feel it in my bones that the ending would be Edwin and Sophie together in happiness. Edwin still tried to hide it, but I knew of every hidden tryst and secretive meeting. I knew of each time Edwin would call off a date with me, only to whisk Sophie off to some fashionable event and shower her with furs and fine jewels. I wasn't supposed to know, and Author kept me from confronting them, but I knew all the same.

To keep the peace, I looked up at the name of the restaurant. "How do you even say the name of this place?" In glowing neon above my head was nothing more than a symbol. Trendy, but impractical.

"Oh, it's so easy." Sophie came up to us. I frowned at the

expensive pink fur coat she wore and the necklace with a diamond the size of a golf ball. How brazen of her to wear Edwin's gifts in front of me.

"My, Sophie, your employer must be paying you well to afford such extravagance," I said.

She giggled, wrapping the coat even more around her. "Oh, these were gifts. Anyway, the name of the restaurant is *eꞇ*."

"*eꞇ* is the best restaurant in town. I often have business meals with multi-million dollar clients here," Edwin said.

"If we get the reception here, it will be the talk of the town," Sophie gushed.

There was no way I'd ever say that name. I could literally see the symbol when they spoke. Just hearing them say the name hurt my ears.

We entered the restaurant and were immediately seated. The waiter smiled and said how lovely it was to have the mother accompany her son and fiancé to the restaurant.

"Gee, I didn't think Sophie looked that old," I said, trying to laugh off the situation.

"No Ma'am. You are the mother," said the waiter.

"Actually, I'm the fiancé," I said.

Edwin sighed. "I'm afraid she's right. She's my fiancé."

"My condolences, sir."

I was sure Author thought this scene was funny, but it was humiliating. And boring. After a while, I was sure the Reader got it: I was ugly and Sophie was pretty. Did the Reader really need to be reminded in nearly every scene?

Edwin and Sophie perused the menu together, their heads nearly touching as they whispered their choices to each other. Anytime Sophie and Edwin got a little too close and nearly kissed, Sophie would blush and pull back slightly. I was surprised that they didn't throw the silverware to the floor and make out on the table top.

"I noticed there were some unauthorized changes to the wedding plans," I said. I kept my eyes on the menu, pretending to not notice their behavior. The menu shook slightly in my hand as Author bore down on me, pushing me to make this a more explosive scene. It took all my strength to keep my voice level. "The flowers were ordered too soon. I thought we agreed to hold off on ordering anything within a color scheme until this situation with the dress has been resolved. Also, the DJ I hired was mysteriously let go and we now have a full orchestra playing at the wedding and reception."

"The wedding colors are pink, cream, and gold. Thus, the flowers need to be pink, cream, and gold," said Sophie.

"My dress, as of the moment, is black and red. You have not produced the copy in pink and cream. Thus, the flowers should not be ordered until we agree on a color scheme."

"It's done," snapped Edwin. "You can't change it, Verucca."

"Au contraire," I said. "For starters, in order to bring about these changes, someone pretended to be me. I noticed these changes because they were charged to me. Using my money without my permission is a crime. I can charge Sophie with felony theft, as the flowers and band cost upwards of a few thousand dollars. Not to mention identity theft."

Sophie gasped. "I did everything to make your wedding perfect! You won't be so cruel as to arrest me for doing my job."

"I will charge you if you touch my money one more time. I

don't care if it's to buy a burger off the dollar menu!"

"But I got your permission. I swear, Edwin, I got her permission. I would never steal." As she said those words, I could feel Author going back and writing in a phone conversation where I, not paying attention to Sophie, did indeed give her permission to use my card as she saw fit for the wedding. The feeling of having one's past rewritten left me a little light headed.

"Verucca, how can you lie about this? Sophie would never steal from you. You must have given her permission. How can you be so mean to her?" Edwin wrapped his arms around Sophie and glared at me.

My eyes locked with Sophie and her "good girl" mask slipped. I could see the cold, calculating look. She knew what she did was wrong, but Author already covered it up. Once she found the perfect way to replace me as the bride, my part would be done.

I, however, came prepared. I pulled a small stack of papers from my purse, secretly pleased that Author had not taken them from me. "This is from my lawyer. A copy, once signed, will be sent to Shirley, one to Edwin, one to Sophie, and I will keep one."

"Exactly what is it," asked Edwin.

"Just a legal document that states that I must have my signature on any and all decisions on this wedding. Not only that, if I am not the bride to walk down the aisle, then I get all money I put into the wedding back effective immediately after the termination of the engagement. That clause, however, also includes the whole shebang; ceremony, reception, and one week of the honeymoon. Also, any purchases made in my name but not with my consent will be paid back immediately by Lovette. I'm sure she won't be thrilled to know she now owes me a few thousand dollars for Sophie's illegal spending."

"This is ridiculous! Why in the world would you feel the need for such a thing?"

With Author bearing down on me, I couldn't tell him the real reason. Author's anger at my underhanded attempt to reign in the Story felt like I was in the middle of the sun and I had to fight my natural inclination to acquiesce and be the Character I was written to be. "I feel it is necessary. I think this little stunt proves my point."

"But you gave me permission," Sophie cried.

"I would have had copies of the changes sent to me and kept better records," I said. "Mysteriously, none of that exists. And it doesn't exist because it was not my call. Be glad I'm not having you arrested, Sophie. Or fired."

"But I did send them to you! Don't you remember giving me permission?" Sophie wrung her hands as she gazed pleadingly at Edwin. "I did everything right. I swear."

"You ordered the wrong flowers. Had you asked me what I wanted, you'd have known that," I said.

"The flowers were the best and most expensive, just what you wanted," she sniffled. She clutched her napkin to her mouth. By now, we were drawing a crowd.

"Expensive doesn't mean in good taste," I said. "You picked out Liscanthias, Lily of the Valley, Hydrangea, and Star Gazer Lilies. I wanted none of those."

"And what disaster did you want," Edwin asked.

"Take out the Liscanthias and cut the Hydrangea population in half. I want none of the lilies at all. Instead, put in roses and carnations. If we go with Sophie's color choices, assuming she finds the dress in time, then the roses can be pink and the carnations can be pink, green, and yellow. Accent it with baby's breath."

"Sounds hideous," Sophie said. "My choice was so much prettier."

"We're sticking to what Sophie picked out. She knows more than you."

"Nothing that she wants mesh well with what I want. I'm the bride, Edwin. It's my wedding and my money. If Sophie wants expensive flowers and a full orchestra, then she can pay for it herself!"

"You're being ridiculous," Edwin snapped. "Jesus, Verucca, if we went with your ideas, the wedding would be a tacky affair by the beach. You should be grateful for all the help Sophie is giving us. Stop acting like a spoiled brat!"

In between sobs, Sophie managed to blurt out, "If that's how you feel, I'll quit."

"See what you've done, Verucca!" He pulled Sophie in the security of his arms. "Don't say that, Sophie. I want you to continue. Verucca is just a cold-hearted, old hag who hates anyone who doesn't think the way she does."

"I want control of my wedding, Edwin. That doesn't make me the bad guy! Stealing my money to plan Sophie's wedding is wrong. For God's sake, I feel as if you're going to use me to fund the perfect wedding and then marry Sophie. You're rich enough to pay for the tasteless affair she wants, so use your own money."

"You're making a scene," Edwin snarled. "Apologize to Sophie."

There was nothing I wanted to do less than apologize to that usurper. My muscles twitched as they strained against

Author's command to debase myself before Sophie. I normally danced to Author's tune, committed any horrible act asked of me, but not this time. I would not go quietly. I did nothing wrong. In the end, the words were ripped from me.

"I am sorry, Sophie. Of course I am grateful for all the work you are doing. I am sure once I see your vision in reality, I will realize how much better it is. Please, ignore my outburst. I must just be hungry to be so mean."

Saying that physically hurt me. I could feel the muscles in my body vibrate with the need to speak my mind, and Author clamped down even more to keep me in line. Sophie brushed away some tears and settled back in her seat. Her face looked none the worse for wear from crying. In fact, if I didn't know better, I'd swear she was faking it. At the triumphant look in her eyes, I wondered what it felt like to have Author on your side.

The rest of the meal was in silence. If I tried to talk, I was chastised. Even in topics not pertaining to the wedding. If I tried to compliment the food, I was told my taste left much to be desired. If I said the night would be cold, I was told it would be warm. When I mentioned that we should have a talk with the priest at the Cathedral, Sophie burst out laughing.

"You're not having a religious wedding. You don't have to talk to anyone."

"But, we are using the Cathedral," I said. "It would only be polite to make sure we know all the rules before having a wedding."

"Verucca! That's enough!" Edwin slammed his hand on the table. "Sophie knows what she's doing!"

Sophie smirked and went back to eating her eight hundred dollar seafood and drinking the wine that was at least two hundred dollars a glass. She knew she was winning.

As we ate dessert (some kind of multi-hundred dollar bowl of mousse with edible gold shavings), Edwin suggested that he'd like to take a trip to his winery, The Dancing Ladies. Sophie jumped at the chance, cooing over the fact that the wine was too expensive for her to have normally and she'd love a chance to taste it.

I stood. "Well, if we are going to The Dancing Ladies, I'd like a chance to clean up a bit. How are we settling the check?"

"I've got it," Edwin said. He did not look pleased, though whether it was because of his volunteering to pay the check or that I believed I was invited along on his little side trip, I wasn't sure. Maybe both.

I left for the bathroom, planning to just do a quick wash up. I held no illusions that they would still be there when I got back. I knew that the invite was only for Sophie, and how rude was it to invite another woman out to the winery in front of your betrothed?

One of the waitresses stopped me at the door. "Do you mind if I ask you something?"

"Shoot."

"You're one of the Mains, right?"

"Yes. I'm the antagonist, I suppose."

She looked at me with sympathetic brown eyes. "This is my first Story. I just…I never thought it could be that bad. I was listening in on the conversation, and you just can't win."

I shrugged. "I'm used to it. I've played the villain almost all my life."

"It's just not fair. It's so obvious what's going on."

"There's nothing I can do."

"I hope you get your chance to be a good guy someday."

~ 80 ~

I smiled. "Me too."

After a quick wash up, I went back to the table. With no surprise, I found it to be empty. Edwin and Sophie ran out without me. I sighed and grabbed my purse. I was almost to the door when a man in an expensive suit stopped me.

"Ma'am, you still have to pay."

"Excuse me?" Please tell me I heard him wrong.

"Ma'am, the bill for your table was not paid. While I am thrilled you and your party chose to eat in my establishment, I must demand payment."

"I thought Edwin paid the bill."

"No, ma'am. Mr. Van Der Woody said you were responsible for payment after your behavior tonight. On that note, I am afraid after this, you are barred from ever setting foot in *et* again, Ms. Tottenstinker."

Humiliation washed over me as I dug in my purse for my card. The bill was so astronomically high it would have been laughable if this weren't such a sad situation. "I see that there are some extra dishes on here?"

"Mr. Van Der Woody got two meals and an extra dessert to go. Please pay."

I handed the card over and heard people whispering behind me. The owner swiped my card personally and presented me with the print out. "Be sure to tip generously."

"I think my meal alone just paid for a new boat," I muttered.

As I handed the paper back to the owner, he whispered, "I am sorry. I knew this scene was coming as soon as that man left. I really did not wish to embarrass you. This whole affair has been horrible for all of us."

"I'm used to it," I said. I felt hot tears in my eyes and

rushed out before anyone could see me cry. I got in my car and told my driver to get me home. As we drove, I dialed Steven's number and got his voicemail.

"Steven, I need to talk to you. When you get this, please call me back."

Maybe, I wasn't as used to this as I thought.

# Planning His Pleasure

The Dancing Ladies Winery sparkled like a fairy land under the light of the full moon, silver moonbeams dancing off the perfect grapes hanging tantalizing off their branches. The sweet scent of Brunello, Merlot, and Dolcetto mingled in the crisp April air with the heady smell of fresh earth. A gentle breeze blew in from Faycrest, and Sophie could imagine that she heard, even from here, the distant noises of life on the wind.

"This is so perfect," Sophie cooed. She plucked a fresh grape and popped in her mouth. With a moan of delight, she turned to Edwin. The moonlight sparkled along her naked skin, still flushed from their recent love-making, making her look like a goddess. Her blonde hair flowed behind her like a halo. She picked a second grape and Edwin watched as her perfect lips wrapped around it before sucking the grape into her mouth with a soft 'pop'.

"This winery is nothing," Edwin said softly. "It's you who makes this moment perfect."

Sophie blushed under the silver moonlight. "Oh, Edwin, I feel so scandalous for what we did. Running out of the restaurant and leaving the bill has to be the most wicked thing I've ever done."

"Verucca had it coming." Edwin went to the cart left next to where they recently made love and grabbed a bottle of wine and two glasses. As he poured, he said, "She's always talking about how she can pay her own way, so why not let her pay. Besides, she deserves it for how she treated you." He brought the wine over to Sophie.

"You are truly my white knight," she said. They stood there, naked as Adam and Eve in their own private Garden of Eden.

"Sophie, there is something I must confess," Edwin said as he finished his glass of wine.

"What is it my love?"

"As hard as it is for me to say this, Verucca was right about one thing."

"What?"

"These last few months have been bliss for me, Sophie. I know Verucca was trying to be mean to you when she said it was like we were planning your wedding, but she had a point. I never picture Verucca walking down the aisle, I picture you. Every facet of what you create has you imprinted on it. You are the princess I want to see coming toward me in a gown of flowing cream and pink. You are the one I picture saying my vows to, the one I want to dance with, the only one I want to wake up to every morning. Even with Verucca tagging along, I picture she is no one and you are the only person I ever need."

Sophie sighed. "Oh, Edwin. I feel the same way. I wish we had met first."

Edwin threw his wine glass into the grove, hearing it shatter among the grape vines. He took Sophie's face in his hands and showered every inch of her in kisses. "I can't stand to be parted from you, Sophie. Tonight has shown me that. You are the only woman for me."

"I know what you mean. This time in the winery has been like heaven. I loved you the moment I saw you, Edwin. I want to rescue you from Tottenstinker. I know she's not the woman for you."

"It's complicated. I would love to leave Verucca, but..." Edwin sighed, pulling Sophie to him. Her silken skin pressed to his and he had to control himself from wanting to make love all over again. "She has something on me, something caused by my own foolishness. She exploited it and this whole wedding is a farce. Verucca is a master when it comes to trapping people in a contract.

*How else do you think she's gotten so many people to buy that awful coffee of hers? And, now she has me. It's unbreakable!"*

*Sophie gasped. "You mean she's blackmailing you? What can she possibly have on a guy who is the most generous and kind person on the face of the planet?"*

*"A mistake from my youth." Edwin took Sophie's hand and led her further into the grove. "Let's not think about Verucca for now. Tonight is all about you."*

*Sophie surrendered to his caresses, but her mind raced. She knew things about Tottenstinker, about how evil she was, and she just could not let Edwin suffer any longer. Sophie would have to save her knight in shining armor!*

# Chapter Eleven

The next morning, I woke up feeling this side of death warmed over. I knew it was because I cried myself to sleep, but it couldn't be helped. Though I was the villain countless times before, this one felt the cruelest. Why give me hope and yank it away? With supreme effort, I pulled myself out of the bed and ambled my way to the bathroom. After a hot shower, I felt like myself again. I faced facts; I knew I was the villain. But, what was I going to do about it? Could I really let this continue and allow Author to control everything, or should I disobey and take back my life?

Downstairs, the door slammed and I heard someone throw something on the table. I pulled my robe on, tying it tightly.

"Steven? Is that you?"

"Yeah. Girl, we need to talk!"

I heard him running up the stairs, possibly taking them two at a time. I towel-dried my hair, waiting. When he entered my room, he was not the normal Steven I grew accustomed. Gone were the bright clothes and spiked hair. Instead, he looked like a different person with his blonde hair smoothed back and somber black clothes on.

"What's going on?"

"Last night I was out on this date. It wasn't going well because, well, I'm not gay and he was. Normally, this is something my wife and I will laugh about in Outer World, but I personally think she's starting to think Author is right. So, I doubt I'll tell her." He took a breath. "Anyway, we were talking over dessert and he kept hinting that he'd like me to come to his place. I really didn't want to. Not just because I'm not in to him, but because I promised my neighbors I'd stop by for movie night."

"What happened?"

"That's when you called. I wanted to pick up, because I knew you'd call either to push the plot forward or because something happened. But, Author forbade me to. I am so sorry I missed your call."

"That's all right." I hung my towel up. "I was upset, but it wasn't anything really major. Just a few more plot points in my face about how I am the wrong woman."

"My date got really nasty after your call, just so you know. Author bore down on us. How can you stand it? Normally, as a Minor Character, I don't get the full heat of Author. But, man, I felt it last night. She wanted me to bad mouth you and turn my back on you."

"Oh, Steven." I sighed. "What happened?"

"I refused. I struggled, but I did the right thing. I stood up for you. It hurt. I never knew it physically hurt to defy Author, but it does. I'm still sore. The important thing is, I stood up for you."

I smiled. "Thank you, Steven. You're my hero."

"You deserve it, Verucca. I know a few of the Background Characters feel the same way. I mean, this Story has you like some mustache-twirling villain about to tie poor Sophie to the railroad tracks. It's that comical."

"It doesn't feel comical from my end."

"I'm sure it doesn't. And I have a feeling I'm about to get a taste of what you've gone through." He ran a hand through his hair. "This morning, I got up to contact my wife..."

"Is she in this Story?"

"No, she's still in Outer World."

"Wait! You can contact Outer World?"

He shrugged. "Yeah. Most my previous Characters were computer hackers. I retained some of the knowledge and figured a way to contact my wife. We talk when either of us is in a Story, though the timing is weird. I mean, months to years can pass in a Story and it's only a few hours in Outer World. It gets real interesting when we're in different Stories."

"You're lucky. The only thing I retained from previous Stories is the looks of horror on the faces of all my victims. Do you know how depressing it is to walk down the street and run into a previous stepdaughter and have her scream in terror at the sight of you? I really wish I could retain some skill but I was never given any skills." I grabbed my clothes for the day and went into the closet. Through the door, I said, "That's one reason why I wanted a Happily Ever After. Just one Story that won't end with me having no friends."

"Aw, Verucca, I'll remain your friend."

I finished getting ready and got out of the closet. We went downstairs and finished our normal morning routine. Something dug at the back of my mind as I mulled over everything that happened in the last twenty-four hours.

As we got ready to leave for the office, I said, "Steven, you use a computer to talk to your wife? I heard you right?"

"Yeah. We talk almost every night."

"Can you look up our backgrounds? Would that be possible?" I was curious to know exactly my history. I felt conflicted as I built a company from scratch and provided a good service, but was expected to be vilified. Was there something I was missing?

Steven thought for a moment. "I can hack Author's

computer and get her manuscript. It won't be complete because it's on-going, but we can use that as a starting point. While I do that, you can look up what the Story says is the background of the Characters."

I nodded. "Something just feels off about this. I'm used to playing one dimensional characters whose only motivation is money or to be pure evil. But, that can't be my motivation here as I have my own money and my only evilness stems from not wanting the same kind of wedding Sophie wants. I have a past."

We rode to the office in silence as neither of us was sure if we could trust my driver. My office was as busy as ever with the typical background work. Earl, the office manager, greeted me and pulled me away for the meetings of that day. Steven trailed behind as my silent shadow.

By lunch, I felt Author bearing down on me. It was time to perform. Under the guidance of Author I called Edwin to confront him over last night. I didn't fight Author because this was something I wanted to do anyway.

After being hung up on three times and put on hold for nearly a half hour, I finally got through to Edwin.

"This better be important, Verucca!" Edwin's voice no longer caused butterflies in my stomach.

"I want an explanation, Edwin. You owe me that much," I said. "What you did was offensive. After you said you would handle the bill, you ran out. Do you have any idea how opprobrious…how utterly humiliating…that was? And not only did you sneak out on the bill, but you left with that Jezebel! I was so embarrassed. They stopped me at the door like a common thief. All because you thought it would be funny to stick me with the check and run off to philander with

Sophie."

"I would say you're blowing it out of proportion, but I can't understand half of what you said."

"I said you humiliated me so you could go off and have sex with Sophie!"

"Really, Verucca, you have such an imagination. All I did was drive her home."

At that moment, Steven placed the morning paper on my desk. He gave me an innocent look before walking off. There, on the front page, was a picture of Sophie and Edwin in the vineyard, canoodling under a blanket and possibly naked. The romantic story was how the pair spent the night at Edwin's winery, making sweet love under the stars.

Tapping the story with my finger, I said, "I have proof that you and Sophie were together. In fact, you were together at your winery. Naked."

I could feel Author trying to stop me, but this was my moment. I was the villain, and I would make Edwin suffer. And nothing hurt more than the truth. If Author didn't want the whole Story to know about Edwin and Sophie, why allow it to be printed?

"Verucca, you're just making things up."

"Have you seen today's paper?"

"What does that have to do with anything?"

"I'll wait. Just look at it."

I heard him call for his paper. I waited patiently as he read the first page. His gasp was fantastically clear and then he handed the paper to someone, whispering just loudly enough for me to hear, "Look at this."

At the feminine screech of outrage, I smiled. "Oh, I see you found the article. Fair warning, Edwin. The next time you plan on cheating on me, please make sure that there are no reporters spying on you. Makes it really hard to lie when I have evidence printed all over the city."

"You had someone follow me!"

"Oh, no, Edwin. As you can see, it's Lorna who wrote the article. No doubt, she was trying to angle for a romantic little piece about you and Cinderella. Too bad she has no clue how to keep her mouth shut." I waved the paper in front of me like a fan. "Be sure to tell Sophie that we will not need her services. It has to be against the contract for the wedding planner to sleep with the groom."

"You are not firing Sophie," Edwin snarled. "She is the only good thing about this wedding."

"I want her gone, Edwin."

"You can't fire her! I won't allow it!"

With the way Author was pushing down on me, I knew that Sophie would not be fired. However, I would not back down so easily. "I can't trust you, Edwin, and I can't trust her. What kind of woman would I be if I allowed Sophie to work with us after I know that you two slept together? In fact, I've half a mind to call the whole thing off."

"You can't!" Was that panic I heard in Edwin's voice? "Please, Verucca, you can't do that. Listen, I'm sorry. It won't happen again. You have my word. I promise. Just...Please don't call off the wedding."

This time I gave in to Author's pestering. "Very well, Edwin. This is your last chance. But if I so much as see any hint of your eyes lingering on Sophie, then it's over."

I hung up and felt Author leave. Slumping in my chair, I felt exhausted. I wasn't sure what had happened, but there was some reason Edwin did not want the engagement to be over. It could just be because Author wanted to use the wedding as some dramatic reveal, but something told me there was more to it. I needed to find that piece of the puzzle, and fast.

"That was amazing!" Steven and Earl came into my office. Steven looked at me in amazement. "You had the upper hand that time."

"Not really. If Author is smart, she'll have Lorna not print any more stories about Edwin and Sophie."

Earl cleared his throat. "Well, if it helps, the newspaper isn't under Author's control. The stories are all Lorna's doing. It was originally to keep the Character's in the loop, but she's gone off and made it her mission to push this Story along."

"And how do you know that," I asked.

"I, um, have a boyfriend in the paper."

Ah, the ever elusive in-Story romance that is not of the plot. Earl looked scandalized, his beady eyes darting up to the ceiling as if he expected Author to appear. This was not the first time I've heard of Background Characters falling in love, and I knew what he feared. If Author ever got wind of it, she might either decide they were not meant to be together and force them apart, or she'd use them in her war against me.

"I won't breathe a word to anyone," I said. "And, thank you for letting me know that Lorna has gone rogue."

Though I feared that my giving away Lorna's article would prevent me from using the paper to spy on Edwin, Lorna's ego proved to be far superior. I never told Edwin of how many times the newspaper printed about him and Sophie. I merely cut the articles out and kept them in a file. Author would not let me end the engagement so soon.

I wondered if Author understood that having the heroine

sleep with a man who had a fiancé was not a desired trait. If anyone should be the cheater, it would be me. I was the villain. And yet, I was the faithful party.

I spent my evenings digging into my background. I had to find the answer to this mystery. Why was I the villain when I did nothing villainous to speak of?

# Chapter Twelve

At the beginning of May, Sophie dragged Edwin and I out for another restaurant review. We decided that *et* would not be our reception site, and she was positive that this place would be perfect. Warning bells went off for me when I heard her say that this was another ultra-expensive restaurant she always wanted to try.

Not that all the previous plans for my wedding weren't also Sophie's choice. Since I was unable to fire her, I was forced to go along with what she wanted. Not even calling up Shirley would work. A few days ago, the three of us went cake tasting. I found out my Character was allergic to banana after being violently ill from three different cakes that featured banana. No surprise, but Sophie just fell in love with the Tropical cake: a banana- and coconut-flavored cake with pineapple filling and banana frosting, covered in toasted coconut.

"The cake will make me sick," I protested. "This would be fine for a groom's cake, but not the main wedding cake."

"But it's perfect. You don't need to eat the cake," Sophie said.

"What about the Pink Champagne? That would fit in just fine with the whole fairytale pink and cream theme."

Sophie shook her head. "Nope. It's the Tropical."

In the end, I lost.

Standing outside the restaurant Sophie wanted to try, I already knew this was not the place to hold a reception. The restaurant was called Lights Out, a kitschy little place where the diners ate in the dark. It marketed that, without the sense of sight, all other senses were heightened. This meant that ordinary food would taste exceptional, and the fine dining they offered would be a treat from the heavens.

"I don't know," I said, peering into the darkness of the restaurant. "People like to dance and mingle at the reception. I don't see that happening here."

"Don't be such a stick in the mud," Edwin said. "You haven't even given this place a chance."

The hostess greeted us at the door and led us into the main dining room. We walked in a line; Edwin's hand on the hostess' shoulder, Sophie holding on to Edwin, a waiter between Sophie and myself. The waiter and hostess wore night vision goggles and were the only ones who could see. Once we were seated, we were told there was no menu. There were three entrée options: Meat, Seafood, and Vegetarian dishes.

"Oh, just like a reception," Sophie cooed. "I'll have the vegetarian option. After all, I'm a vegetarian."

"How responsible of you," Edwin declared. "I find it admirable that you care so much about the helpless animals."

I bit my tongue. Vegetarian my bony butt. At the last restaurant, little Miss Vegetarian was chowing down on duck and seafood.

"What comes on the platters?" I asked.

"Well, the vegetarian platter comes with a salad made with Matsutake mushrooms and Kabu turnips, imported from Japan, and Romanian carrots, dressed in a white truffle oil infused with hop shots and saffron. The main dish is fried tofu in an artichoke and black truffle soup. It's extremely popular and considered our bestselling dish."

"That sounds divine," Sophie said with a sigh.

"And the other dishes," I asked.

"There goes Verucca, slaughtering innocent creatures," Edwin muttered

"If we are really considering this place for the reception, we should not evade our duty by only ordering one kind of dish. They offer three different platters, we should each order one. Sophie is ordering the vegetarian dish, so that means the other two of us should order the meat and seafood."

"I'm getting the vegetarian platter." Edwin sniffed. "I won't hurt an animal. But, knowing your job, you hurt animals all the time."

"I pass inspection every time," I said. "I couldn't do that if I abused my animals."

"That's because she uses bribery." Sophie whispered loudly enough for me to hear her. "My friend, Heather, is this close to busting the Cat Camp wide open."

"That's wonderful." Edwin didn't bother whispering.

"The other two platters," I repeated. "Can anyone tell me what comes on them?"

"Oh, um, chicken is our meat dish. You get half a chicken, dressed in Asian spices, with a chestnut mousse and a caviar parfait appetizer. Our seafood option is butter poached lobster paella served with scallops and tangerines and a mini pizza appetizer with lobster and three kinds of caviar."

"I'll have the chicken, please," I said. I was not sure if the combinations they were serving would taste good together, but I was not going to starve myself. Plus, if I was to be Sophie's opposite, it only made sense for me to eat the meat dish.

After the waiter took our order and left, there was no

conversation. I tried a few times to talk about what we really wanted in a reception hall, but no one answered me. Thanks to the dark, I was acutely aware of what Sophie and Edwin were really up to. It was hard to ignore the obscene noises of them kissing, moaning, and the rustle of clothing being moved around so one or the other could caress skin.

People around us could hear them, too. Their conversations washed over me, adding to the anger I felt over this newest treatment.

"That's the Mains over there? Sounds like a cheap romance to me." A woman to my left was whispering.

"Weren't there three people who came in? Maybe a kinky erotica?" That sounded like a man at the same table.

"I don't think so. I saw them in the lobby. One is definitely not romance material."

From my right, I heard, "What is the direction of the Story? Why put in a fiancé if all the focus is on the two pretty people?"

"Not sure. I almost forgot there was a fiancé. Everything we hear is about the one guy and girl."

I could also hear the hostess and the waiter. They commented on how hot and heavy Sophie and Edwin were getting. At Sophie's low, breathless moan, I heard the hostess say, "Should we break them up?"

"Normally, yes, but I'm rooted to the spot," the waiter replied. "Geez, they are practically naked."

"I thought the engagement was the guy and the other girl?"

"Not really. I've kept up to date on the news articles, and it's really driving it home that this is the intended couple."

The hostess sighed loudly. "Must suck to be her."

I had enough. I raised my arm to call the waiter over. However, when I felt him step up next to me, he wasn't there to answer my call.

"I am sorry to intrude, but there is a gentleman caller here for Miss Sophie Winslow. He's in the lobby and says it's important."

There was a rustle of clothes. "Oh, I'll go see who it is." Sophie's chair scraped back and I heard her walk off, her heels clipping smartly on the floor.

"I should head to the men's room," Edwin said. Before I could say anything, he pushed his chair back and stumbled out. I heard the waiter rush after him.

I waited until I heard the chair next to me move again. "Edwin, we need to talk. Despite the darkness in here, I'm not blind. Nor am I deaf. I know what's going on between you and Sophie. In fact, everyone in here knows. I can't believe you would do this to me. After all your promises, you embarrass me by making out with Sophie. That's it, Edwin. I've had it. The engagement is off."

"Uh, ma'am, I'm not your fiancé." It was the waiter. "I came to tell you that Mr. Van Der Woody has left with his lady friend. They took their orders to go. I can bring you a to-go bag or you can finish your meal at the table."

"I don't suppose he paid for the meal?"

"No, ma'am. I can bring you the bill."

I laid my head down on the table. Author must thought this was funny, always sticking me with the bill, but it was getting old. Edwin was not the romantic hero. He was a cheater. Sophie was not a rags to riches story. She was the other woman. And, somehow, they were supposed to be the Main Characters. They would get a Happily Ever After, while

I guessed my ending would be dubbed, "Alone Forever".

I paid and got my meal to go. As I walked out into the lobby, I waited a moment for my eyes to adjust to the light. When they did, I spotted a man standing at the far end of the lobby. He watched the people coming out, obviously looking for someone.

The man was of average height with ordinary brown hair with a mullet style. He wore a stained white shirt and dingy jeans. Over the shirt was an equally stained denim, long-sleeved work shirt with a name tag. His hands still smudged from dirt and calloused from hard work. He looked out of place in the lobby of this fancy restaurant.

"That's the man who came in for Miss Sophie," the hostess whispered to me. "She took one look at him and asked us to sneak her out the back. She was met by Mr. Van Der Woody and they left through the alley.

Whoever this gentleman was, Sophie didn't want anything to do with him. Author hovered over us in a cloud of oppression, pushing for some scene between the man and myself. For a moment, our eyes met and he raised one hand in a shy wave. I felt like I knew him, but I couldn't recall ever meeting him before.

Walking over, I held out my hand. "I'm Verucca Tottenstinker. I understand you're looking for Sophie Winslow. What business do you have with her?"

He shook my hand vigorously. "I'm Bob Smith. I'm Sophie's boyfriend. We were supposed to go out for our anniversary tonight, but when I got home from work, all I found was a note saying she was out with her clients."

I looked over his filthy clothes. Now that I was closer I could tell they were mechanic's clothes. Some of the dark dirt stains were really oil and grease smudges. "I take it you didn't stop to change?"

"Um, no ma'am. I felt compelled to hurry over here." He peered back into the inky blackness of Lights Out. "Is Sophie in there?"

"She's left. I'm afraid you just missed her."

Bob looked down, scuffing his sneakers on the floor. "You know, she's spending a lot of time with you and your fiancée. She's incredibly involved with your wedding. It's eating up all her time. I just wanted us to have a nice night out, and I guess that's not going to happen."

"I assure you, had I known she had other plans, I would have insisted she kept them," I said. "I personally don't think we need the wedding planner to help us decide what restaurant to pick, but Edwin is just...enamored with her."

"She's pretty wrapped up with him, as well." Bob sighed, turning to the door. "Sorry to have interrupted your night, Ms. Tottenstinker. If you see Sophie, please let her know I was looking for her."

"I will. Have a nice night, Bob." I walked away from him. All I could think was, Poor guy. With a plain name like Bob Smith, he must a throw-away Character. Author did not waste any brain cells with him.

# Planning His Pleasure

"Sophie! Wait!" Edwin chased after his beautiful angel as she ran through the city streets. Something back at Lights Out frightened her, and he barely had enough time to grab their to-go boxes and follow as she scampered out into the night. "Sophie!"

She finally stopped, collapsing several blocks away from the restaurant in a park. Her blonde hair was in disarray, partly from their make out session and partly from her mad flight. She knelt there, trying to catch her breath.

"Sophie? What's going on? Why did you run away?" Edwin sat next to her, his hand on her back in comfort. "Who was that disgusting man?"

"Oh, Edwin! It's just too awful!" Sophie clung to him, trying to not sob. "I didn't expect him to come after me. He's just so possessive!"

"Who?"

"My boyfriend, Bob Smith." Sophie choked on a sob. "We've been dating for nearly two years now and he keeps getting worse. At first, I thought his possessive nature was charming. It was just romantic how he would call me his. But then, he started showing his true colors and he frightened me. Then, I got my wonderful job and my paychecks were more than his. He grew jealous and started putting me down. He doesn't make enough working the menial jobs his uneducated self can get, and that's only when he is working. He's often unemployed and living off my paychecks!" She buried her head in the crook of Edwin's neck and burst into fresh tears.

"Do you love him?" Edwin's heart sank at the thought of his beautiful Sophie belonging to another man.

"No. I used to, but that love faded long before we met. I love only you, Edwin."

"Does he beat you?"

She shook her head. "No, but I can tell it's only a matter of time. He...He raised his voice to me the other day!"

Edwin scooped her up in his arms. "Don't you worry, Sophie. I won't let anything happen to you."

Sophie sniffled. "What am I going to do, Edwin? He'll be waiting for me at home."

"I know! You can stay at one of my many, private apartments. I keep them on the side in case I need to hide from Verucca. You can stay there for free, and this Bob Smith will never find you."

"What about Verucca?"

"What about her?"

"I fear she'll try to harm me, too. She's shown to have such a temper and she will do anything to keep us apart."

"You leave her to me. I won't let her or anyone else ever cause you harm." Edwin kissed Sophie. "No one will ever hurt you again."

"What about when you marry her?"

Edwin smiled. "As I said, she knows nothing about my secret apartments. You'll be safe. And I have a feeling I'll spend all my time with you rather than her." He shuddered. "Can you imagine being married to such a bony creature?"

"But you'll be married!"

Edwin heaved a dramatic sigh, letting Sophie down so she could stand. "I don't want to marry her. I must, for the sake of my company. If I knew a way around it, I'd leave her for good."

They started walking in the park, holding hands and enjoying the company of the other. Sophie only wanted Edwin. Like him, she was stuck in her relationship. She tried to leave Bob several times, but he always tricked her to get her to come back. He alternated between threatening harm to himself and stalking her until she returned. He was such a filthy brute. Nothing like her dear Edwin.

Edwin stopped. "Sophie, there is something I want to give you," he said. He pulled out his keychain and swiftly took off a key. "Here. It's to my main home. Any time you want, just show up. I'll let the doorman know that you are always welcomed. And this one," he took off another key, "is to my apartment on East Street. It's not far from here. You can live there until we figure all this out. It's furnished, and I will buy you a new wardrobe so you don't have to go home again."

"Oh, Edwin! This is so sudden!"

"Please, say you'll stay safe. I couldn't bear it if anything happened to you."

Sophie smiled and took the keys. "I will, Edwin. Thank you so much for looking out for me. I love you."

# Chapter Thirteen

For the next two weeks, I barely spoke to Edwin. When I tried to talk about the incident at Lights Out, he gave me excuse after excuse. I didn't understand Sophie. I was too mean. I could afford to pay once in a while. No apologies. No promises to never abandon me again. Nothing that a loving fiancée would say. I watched sadly as the last thread of my Happily Ever After faded away.

I spent my time studying my Character. I was not popular in school, lived most of my life in a small town, and started Tabby Pops Coffee while in college. Most of this I already knew. What I didn't know was that I sent a good portion of my profits back to the town I grew up in. That was something to look into.

The week before Memorial Day, Sophie called me to tell me that she found the dress in pink and cream. If I wanted it, I would have to get it fast. Even though it was the perfect dress, Sophie was not going to go out of her way to ensure I had it. After all, as the villain, I was expected to ruin her wedding plans, and thus keep the black dress.

I rushed to the wedding shop, praying that the dress was still there. Luck was on my side and it was not only still there, but it was the perfect fit.

"This must be an incredibly popular dress," the sales girl told me. "At least three other people called on this dress. All of them wanted to buy it sight unseen. I turned them down."

"Because it was on hold for me?"

"Well, no. Officially, it wasn't put on hold. When we

received the call from Miss Sophie, she merely asked about it. But, I figured if a Main was asking, it was important and should be kept until a Main could come in and see it."

"Thank you," I said. I smoothed my hands down the dress. "You have no idea what this means to me." I still loved the black and red version, but this one would finally get Edwin off my back for ruining 'dear Sophie's' dream wedding. Maybe I could wear the black and red version to the reception dinner or to some charity event?

"I want you to know I stood up for you," the sales girl said. "Author didn't want you to have this dress and it was hard to keep it here. Be careful."

"Can you have it secretly delivered to my apartment," I asked. "I can carry out an empty box, just in case anything is supposed to happen."

The sales girl nodded. "I can. But if Author is determined to ruin this dress, empty box or not, it will be ruined."

"I will be careful."

The sales girl started to box the dress. "I've been following the Story through those news articles. I really felt sorry for you. You don't deserve all of this." She looked up at me and smiled. "You don't recognize me, do you?"

When I shook my head no, she pulled her hair to a one-sided ponytail. "Oh! Three years ago, when I played that corrupt orphanage director! You were the heroine's best friend."

"Right, I played Sarah."

This was a bit awkward. Normally, when I ran into any of the protagonists of my past Stories, they did not want to talk about the past. I was the villain, and that was all that mattered. It brought back too many bad memories.

"Listen, I wanted to hate you," Sarah said. "You were rather despicable in that Story. I mean, the whole abusing children and stealing money and selling the heroine to a biker gang, it was just awful. I really wanted to hate you."

"I'm not really like that," I protested.

"I know that now. You see, I was recently in a Story where I was a villain, too. The things I was forced to do…I'm going to have nightmares for a long time. And the worst part, one of my victims was my little brother. I thought he would understand, but when we got back to Outer World, he won't talk to me or have anything to do with me. He only sees that Character. He won't even go to therapy with me." She sighed. "So, it made me realize that we are not our Characters. I'm not that evil woman who tortured my brother. I'm me. And when I saw that you were in this Story, it made me remember how I felt and I got to thinking that maybe you were the same."

I felt tears prickling in my eyes. "Thank you. You're the first person from my past to see that."

She handed me an empty box. "You'd best be on your way. I don't know how long Author will be gone, but I don't want to be caught helping you when she comes back."

I nodded and took my empty box. While growing up, I was taught that Author always knows all. I was hoping that was false and Author only knew what he or she was focusing on at that moment. Maybe Author will be so enthralled with whatever Sophie and Edwin were up to that I would have a reprieve.

Since it was such a lovely day out, and Sunday to boot, I decided to enjoy the good weather. I stopped off at a little cafe for lunch, watching the people. I imagined what they must be thinking, as Background Characters. Suddenly, the hairs on the back of my neck stood on end. Why were there so many Background Characters milling about? It wasn't for my benefit. Just as I realized that there were too many people, I felt Author's presence. She wasn't focused on me, but I knew that Sophie and Edwin were near-by.

Sure enough, I spotted them across the street, peering into a jewelry shop. Sophie was pointing happily at the various wares. I pulled out my phone and dialed Edwin's number, watching him. He took one look at his phone and ignored it, sending me to his voice mail.

Hanging up, I paid for my meal. I decided to spy on my fiancée and see for myself what he was up to. Despite my intent to spy, I didn't bother hiding myself as I crossed the street. If they saw me, then I could easily turn this into an accidental meeting. After all, the dress shop wasn't too far from here for it to be impossible for me to remain in this area.

They walked down the street, away from me, and entered a small cafe. In the back was an elevated deck for eating with a view of a park. I heard Edwin ask for a seat on the deck. I quickly went down the nearest alley, planning on listening in to their conversation. From where I stood, I could hear them as plain as day.

"Oh, Edwin," simpered Sophie in her breathless voice. "This is just the most adorable cafe ever. Of course, everything with you is just the best."

"I can't wait until every day is like this, my love," Edwin gushed. "You're like a breath of fresh air."

"I still haven't thanked you properly for taking me out to that wonderful restaurant last night. Or for the gorgeous diamond necklace."

Edwin chuckled. "My dear, you thanked me plenty in

bed."

I ground my teeth at Sophie's air-headed giggle. I was no longer surprised or disappointed at the fact that they were seeing each other. I just wished to leave the Story and get on with my life.

"My God, Sophie, I love being with you. I love being able to be myself around you. All those stuffy social events and high society charities are all Verucca's doing. She constantly needs the spotlight. But not you. You are content to be yourself and let everyone admire the real you. I appreciate that."

I needed the spotlight? Little Mr. and Miss Front Page News did nothing to stop Lorna's stories about their affair. They always picked the priciest places in town and were now flaunting their affair in public.

"Edwin, darling, why don't we elope? Let's leave all our troubles behind and get married. We can move to some exotic island. You can do your work through the computer, if need be."

Edwin sighed dramatically. "I would if I could. You know that, Sophie. But with Verucca's blackmail hanging over my head, I just can't. That cold-hearted vulture would swoop in and take my business if I ran off with you."

My ears perked up. Blackmail? That was news to me.

"But, it's just her word against yours. Who would believe that ugly old hag over you anyway?"

"Alas! She has a contract in her possession. She can prove that I am bound to her by marriage in exchange for my company."

I made a mental note to find this contract. I was pretty sure it would prove to be illegal, and it if that was all that was keeping me here, I had to find a way to break it.

I started to back away from my hiding spot as Sophie and Edwin talked about how perfect their lives together would be. I was halfway out of the alley when a huge hand clamped down over my mouth from behind. My scream was lost in a flabby wall of flesh.

My assailant spun me around and shoved me against the alley wall. I found myself now facing Bob Smith. He motioned for me to be quiet and hesitantly took his hand away from my mouth.

"What are you doing here?" I whispered.

"Not here. Follow me." He motioned and walked out of the alley. Feeling like I had no other choice, I followed him.

# Chapter Fourteen

Bob and I went across the way to the little park. The air hung heavy between us, but neither one wanted to start the conversation. For a moment, we silently watched the ducks swimming peacefully in a small man-made pond.

"So, how long have you known," Bob asked.

"About Edwin and Sophie? Since the beginning. They are not secretive about it at all," I said. "You?"

"A little bit after. I gave Sophie the benefit of the doubt. I thought that Edwin was going to be an obstacle in our path, but I came to realize I was the obstacle."

I smiled a bit. "What a sorry pair we are. Both of us are supposed to be blind to the truth, but it's so obvious."

"Especially with that Lorna printing their activities every day."

I groaned. "Don't get me started on Lorna. At least you've escaped her notice."

Bob sighed. "You know, when I first woke up in this Story, I was confused. This isn't how I look in Outer World. When I got a good look at myself, I had a feeling I wasn't in for a Happily Ever After. Or, if I was, it would be as a sidekick. But that doesn't mean I like being played for the fool."

"I know what you mean. When I woke up, I thought this would be my Happily Ever After. I mean, it had all the markings of a good Story. I was rich and self-made, there was no abuse on my part, and I had Edwin. But, as the Story progressed, I quickly learned I was not the heroine. I really hate being the villain. This was just sneaky and I honestly feel as if my dreams were crushed."

"I'm really sorry," Bob said.

"I thought, maybe, this was an Ugly Duckling Story. I know I'm not heroine material. I know I'm ugly. I've had it pointed out since my first Story. But all I ever wanted was my Happily Ever After. Just once. Is that too much to ask?"

"You're not ugly," Bob said. He grabbed my hands. "Listen to me, you're not ugly. I don't care what all those Authors said, they are wrong. You may not be romance novel beautiful, but you are not ugly. You are one of the most confident and kind women I've ever met."

I blushed at his words. "You just met me," I muttered. "How can you know what I'm like?"

"Trust me." He got up. "I'm going to get some bread to feed the ducks. Don't run off." He left and I saw him walk over to a bread vendor. I wanted to run, but where would I go. I would still be in this Story.

I wondered if Bob and I met before. He said he doesn't look like this in Outer World. It was rare, but sometimes our natural appearance reminded an Author of someone they knew, and they'd change our looks for any number of reasons. The biggest would be spite. Bob could remind Author of someone she knew and was mad at, and change his looks as revenge. But, what did he normally look like? When he sat next to me, I tried to picture him as someone else, but all I saw was Bob.

"So, what kind of Characters do you normally play," I asked.

Bob grinned. "The hero. Mostly in paranormal romances. I've been an alpha werewolf, and cat, and vampire, and so on. Even played an angel once. I know I don't look like it, but in

Outer World, I'm actually quite the hottie."

"This is what I normally play." I threw some bread crumbs to the ducks. "I always play the evil stepmother or the villainous other woman or some kind of abuser."

"I know. Too bad all our roles are based on our looks and not our real personalities. Otherwise, I know you'd be a great heroine."

"Stop flattering me. I can't remember if we ever met, so I can't tell if you're joking."

Bob shrugged. "Okay." He watched the ducks eat the bread. "We are raised to serve Author. That is our only purpose in life. If we serve Author well, we can earn our own Happily Ever After. Isn't that the fairytale we are told?"

"I'm beginning to wonder about that," I confessed. "I have done everything asked of me, but I doubt I'll get my Happily Ever After. Sometimes, I doubt Author even knows we're real. What if Author thinks we are products of his or her imagination? How can we earn a Happily Ever After then?"

"Happily Ever Afters are over-rated anyway. Personally, I like the semi-happy endings as a Sidekick or Background Character. You run into a lot less problems in Outer World that way."

"What kind of problems?"

Bob tossed some more bread to the ducks. "Many years ago, I played a prince in a Story that I'm positive was shelved. Anyway, I make it back to Outer World, flushed with my victory. The princess of the Story hunted me down, convinced that we were meant to be. I didn't know better, and we got married. Then, a year or so down the road, she leaves me. Partly because she found another hero and partly because I came to realize that I didn't love her."

"There are cautions all over Outer World about falling for the Character you meet."

"I didn't think anything would happen. The Will of Author and Author knows best kind of thing." Bob sighed. "When we broke up, I realized that it wasn't the princess I loved all along."

"Oh? Who did you love?"

"The villain." He smiled, crumpling up the empty bread bag. "I paid close attention to the villains of my Stories after that. They often turned out to be the nicest people. In a Pirate Story I was in a while back, the evil pirate and I had tea almost every day when Author wasn't looking. We talked about life and fate and what lies beyond Outer World. I've remained friends with many of the bad guys from my Stories."

"That's good of you," I said. "I still want my Happily Ever After. Who knows when I'll ever get another chance? I just want one so I can hold on to the memory of once, just once, there was a Story where people cared about me."

"I suppose that makes sense," Bob said. "I have to go. Just think about what I said. And, do me a big favor. When you get home, look in the mirror and find something you like about yourself. Please, Verucca."

"Okay, I will give it a try."

I stayed in the park a while longer. When I went home, I found my dress waiting for me and in pristine condition. I did look in the mirror. Instead of focusing on my flaws, I tried to find something I liked about myself. In the end, I decided I liked my smile. It wasn't perfect, but when I honestly smiled, I could see myself light up.

So, I like my smile.

I spent Memorial Day pouring over background

information. Edwin was always rich. His parents were multi-millionaires before he was born. He attended only the most prestigious schools, skipped grades due to his genius, and passed top of his class. For some undisclosed reason, his parents handed the company over to him at the age of eighteen and retired to a private island. Edwin, being the genius he was, already had made a name for himself in the business world as the youngest entrepreneur and youngest person to graduate college. Somehow, he managed to get a Master's in business in only two years. It was clear Author paved the way for him to be a success story. He opened the winery when he turned twenty-one, and it was naturally a success. We met three years ago at a charity event, started dating two years ago, and got engaged this year. I found no mention in his background about blackmail, nor could I find any evidence on my end. I even dug out all the scrapbooks and diaries I could find around my apartment and poured over them. Nothing.

Sophie came from a well-to-do family in the same small town I grew up in. She was extremely popular and made good grades. Surprisingly, she was not prom queen our senior year, but she was valedictorian. She dated the star quarterback until she graduated. She went to college, but didn't study anything. She graduated with a General Studies degree, worked menial jobs for a while until she was "discovered" by Shirley Lovette. Since then, she's become a rising star in the wedding business. She dated Bob Smith for two years.

Bob Smith didn't exist. He had no background. His only job in the Story was to date Sophie. Sometimes he had a job, sometimes he was unemployed. Sometimes he was a drunk, sometimes he was sober. He was whatever Author needed at that time. I knew what that was like.

The next day, I entered my office with the intent of searching for the blackmail contract. If I knew my Character, she would be the kind to keep such a thing close. This was the first time that Steven did not meet me at my apartment and drove in with me. Instead, I found him already at the office, setting up a small room next to the elevators with chairs and coffee.

"Something tells me that I forgot something important," I said.

"Interviews today," Steven said. He was once again dressed in somber colors, but his tie was bright vivid green. Frankly, I liked this look more than the loud neon colors. "Remember, we are interviewing for my assistant?"

"Oh, right. Slipped my mind completely."

Steven scooped some coffee into the machine. "I hope you don't mind, but I am putting out a sampling of our coffee. I thought it would be a nice touch if they got to taste the product since most of the Characters can't afford it on their own."

I knew Author would want me to be mad. This was squandering our product on the plebeians who could only dream of tasting such a divine roast. But, Author wasn't around right now.

"That sounds like a plan. I'm glad you thought of it, Steven. As always, you've gone above and beyond expectations. When you're done, come on in my office. I would appreciate your take on each applicant." I left him and assigned a random office girl to hand out the applications and be a guide to the applicants. Earl would take them from the room and bring them to my office when the time was right.

When I got to my office, I noticed Steven left a file of potential applicants on my desk. These should be the people sent in by Author. I wasn't interested in them right now, and began to look through my desk for any blackmail contract. I found nothing by the time Steven joined me.

"The file is on the desk, Ms. Tottenstinker," he said and I felt Author swoop in. It was show time.

"Yes, I was looking for something else." I picked up the file and idly flipped through the applicants. From what I could see, they all looked competent. I read over the resumes until it was time to start interviewing. Earl brought in the first girl and the process started.

To my surprise, the applicants did not seem eager to interview. They were either hostile when they came in, or burst into tears in the middle of the interview. One girl ran out sobbing that she just couldn't do this. I had a feeling that something was amiss.

"There wasn't another Lorna story in the paper this morning, was there?" I looked up at Steven, puzzled at the reactions of the applicants.

"Not that I saw." Steven left the room to check on the remaining applicants. He returned a few minutes later with Earl. "We have one last applicant, and you won't believe who it is."

"Sophie?"

"No. But close. I'll go get her," Earl said.

"Be prepared for a headache," Steven said.

I looked at the name of the last applicant. Lacey Pearl did not sound like anyone I knew, but when she walked in, I recognized her immediately. Lorna Bailey. The dark wig and over-sized glasses did nothing to hide her identity. Especially when she still wore her press pass.

I cleared my throat. "So, um, Lacey Pearl is it?" I made a show of looking over her resume and taking her application from Earl. It was only now that I noticed her references were Heather, Sophie, and Shirley, and "Tottenstinker Stinks" under her skills. I could only imagine that Author wanted her here for this to get past us.

"Yes, I'm Lacey Pearl," she said.

"And you wish to work for Tabby Pops Coffee?"

"With all my heart. I never wanted to work anyplace else. It is a big dream of mine. You're my hero, Ms. Tottenstinker."

Laying it on a bit thick, I thought. I pretended to jot down a note on her resume. "And did you try the coffee we have out in the waiting room? It may be your only chance to sample the product."

She giggled. "Of course I sampled it. I just couldn't pass up a chance like that."

"What did you think?"

"I hate to say this, but it was awful. You can tell it was from a litter box."

Well, since this was Lorna, I took her complaint with a grain of salt. Again, I pretended to make a note.

"I hope my honesty doesn't count against me," she said quickly.

"No, it won't. As part of the assistant job, you will be expected to keep track of the sales records. Right now, I bounce ideas off of Steven. He or I may bounce ideas off of you. Your input, should you get the job, would be valuable to me."

She smiled, pleased with that answer.

"Now, the job is only part-time to help alleviate the burden on Steven," I said. "It's not all that glamorous, but you will be compensated and we do offer a benefits package for part timers. You'll be expected to do the main filing and note-taking duties, along with some travel between here and the Cat Camp. Would you be able to do that?"

"I can do all of that. I have six years of administrative experience."

I was sure that was a lie.

"Could you pass a background check? All of my employees must be trusted, so I want to make sure that there is nothing in your past that will tempt you in the future to give away our secrets."

"I could easily pass a background check."

"Are you sure, Ms. Lacey Pearl, that you could pass?"

"Of course. Why wouldn't I?"

"I don't think you could," I said. I dropped her resume and application in the mini-shredder at my feet.

Lorna looked confused. "What?"

"I said I doubt you could pass a background check. After all, Lacey Pearl doesn't exist. Or, at least, if she does exist, she's not you."

"I don't know what you're talking about. I'm Lacey Pearl!"

"No you're not. You are that prevaricator reporter who writes such tarrididdle at that catchpenny paper intent on maligning my good name. Whatever your true intent, I can guess it's to gather more ammunition for your latest diatribe against me and mine. Your incursion into my building can be seen as a direct attack, and I will not kowtow to what your presence suggests."

"What? Was any of that English?"

"For a reporter, your vocabulary is woefully lacking. You

only spout a verbigeration of garbage in an effort to appease the lowest common denominator. Invest in a thesaurus. Now, I am a busy woman and have indulged you for far too long. I suggest you take your leave." With that, I walked over and yanked off her wig. Lorna gave an undignified squeal, reaching up as if she were bald. Realizing the game was up, she glared at me.

"Exactly what did you just say to me? I demand to know!"

"You are a liar, who writes for a horrible paper that cares nothing about quality. You have a low vocabulary, and I am tired of dealing with you. You have five seconds to leave my office and be on your way or I will call security."

"You won't get away with this, Tottenstinker! I know your true plans!" She jumped up and pointed dramatically at me.

"Five," I said.

"You won't harm Sophie! She's protected by Edwin, and you know it. In fact, they are living together in one of his secret apartments!"

"Four."

"You just want to hurt Sophie again! Wasn't high school enough for you? Why must you hunt us down to ruin our lives?"

"Three." I placed my hand on the phone.

"No one will come! They don't want to work for one as evil as you! You're just a common kitty killer!"

"Two. Really Lorna, just leave."

"That's all you ever do, Tottenstinker. You hide behind others, but we all know what a witch you are. Edwin would be so much happier with Sophie!"

"One." I pushed the button for security. Almost at once, the line was picked up. "Yes, I have an intruder in my office by the name of Lorna Bailey. Please come up and escort her out."

"I told you no one was coming! You can't scare me. I have the truth on my side!"

Three guards came into my office and forced Lorna to leave. She continued to scream that I was in the wrong and she was right, that I would never hurt Sophie, and that Edwin didn't love me all the way down the hall and onto the elevator.

I sat back down, rubbing my temples. "That was the last?"

"Yep," said Steven.

"Oh, good. I need a break."

"We found no assistant," Steven said.

I sighed. Back to square one. Later, we found out what went gone terribly wrong. The sign that should have said, "Waiting room for Assistant Position" now read, "Waiting room to replace Steven". At last, I had my answer for why the interviews didn't go as planned. Author changed the sign behind my back, turning my good deed into a vile attempt to screw over my faithful assistant.

# Planning His Pleasure

Sophie smiled angelically as she retrieved the perfect soufflé from the oven. It was girls' night, and she was making dinner at Heather's home. This would be her first night without Edwin in a long time. Not that she was complaining. Every night with Edwin was heaven, but he said he needed a night off to go over some business that piled up. He also found out that his repulsive fiancé, Verucca Tottenstinker, was seen at the park with another man! How horrible for him to learn that the woman who was blackmailing him into marriage couldn't even be faithful to him. Poor Edwin.

"I just don't get it," said Heather as she set the table. "Why would Tottenstinker cheat on Edwin? He's just too perfect. There is no way any other guy out there could possibly compare."

"Who knows why that old hag does anything," said Lorna. She started pouring their glasses of wine. "Can you believe what she did today? It was just disgusting!"

"What did she do?" asked Sophie.

Lorna looked embarrassed for a moment. Sophie was just too sweet and innocent to be brought into all the drama Tottenstinker created. Lorna regretted bringing the ugly woman up, but as Sophie batted her adorable baby blue eyes, Lorna felt her resolve fail. It was best if Sophie knew what her rival was capable of, just to be prepared.

"She was giving interviews today to replace her assistant. Steven's worked for her since the beginning, and she's planning on tossing him away like trash. And to make matters worse, he was forced to help find his replacement!" Lorna picked up her glass and took a huge swig of her wine. Slamming the glass down on the counter, she said, "And when I tried to ask her questions about it, she threw me out!"

"What else could we expect of her?" asked Heather.

Sophie, seemingly unaffected by this, served the soufflé. As with everything about Sophie, this was just the best soufflé her friends ever tasted. "Sadly," Sophie said, "Tottenstinker is just one of those people who never change. She got her kicks hurting people in high school, and now she continues to get a thrill out of hurting people. After what she did to me at prom and ruining my life..." Sophie sniffled. "I honestly thought she'd recognize me when she saw me at the wedding office, but she must not ever care about the people she must step on to get her way."

"She doesn't notice anything that doesn't benefit her," Lorna said.

Sophie sighed deeply. "And now, she's hurting dear, sweet Edwin. She's probably out trying to butter up some rich business rival of his for more money in her pocket."

Lorna looked down at her plate. "Sophie, it pains me to tell you this, but she wasn't seen with some rich old man. The person Tottenstinker was at the park with was Bob. He's cheating on you."

Large tears filled Sophie's innocent eyes. Her beautiful pink lips trembled. "He's what? Oh, no! After all I've done for him!" She pushed her plate out of the way as she set her head on the table and cried. "He promised he wouldn't do that anymore. I'm such a good girlfriend to him! How can he cheat on me?"

"Why don't you just leave Bob? I mean, Edwin will take care of you. You can kick that cheater to the curb." Heather patted Sophie on the head.

"But what did I ever do to deserve to be cheated on?"

Lorna's eyes glittered with unshed tears of sympathy. "I know. Let's get back at Bob. He can't hurt you like this, Sophie. He and Tottenstinker are just evil people, and you can't let them win."

"Bob isn't hurting you, is he," asked Heather.

Sophie nodded and stood up. She lifted her pink shirt to reveal a large bruise along the right side of her hip.

"Oh, Sophie! What happened?"

"I was grabbing some of my things from the apartment the other day when Bob came home early. Fired from his job and drank away his paycheck, as usual. When he saw me, he came at me and I tried to run. I tripped and fell against the edge of a table." She started to sob. "He told me to get out! I should have known he found someone else."

Heather pulled Sophie in a hug. "Let Tottenstinker keep him. They deserve each other."

Lorna joined the hug. "Yeah. Those two are like peas in a pod. You have Edwin now. He loves you."

Sophie sighed deeply again. "I just wish I knew how Tottenstinker is blackmailing Edwin. He won't confide in me the details. It makes me feel like he's keeping secrets, like he can't trust me." She gave her friends a watery smile. "I guess that's just Bob's betrayal talking. I mean, finding out the boyfriend you gave two years of your life to just up and cheated on you with your mortal enemy..."

"You're too good for the likes of Bob. You are moving up, Sophie," said Heather. "You have a beautiful penthouse apartment that you practically share with Edwin. You have Edwin, who can support you and take care of all your needs. I bet he's a better lover than Bob, too. You have everything now. Just cut Bob loose. He'll figure out what he's missing when he's living on the streets. I doubt Tottenstinker will take him in."

"I love Edwin so much." Sophie smiled. "Between us girls, the fact that I'm the one he's picking over Tottenstinker just makes it all the more sweet. And Edwin has promised that he'll find a way to marry me someday. And I'll never have to work again. I'm sure I can find a way to spread the wealth to you two, for all you've done for me. He's got some really handsome single friends."

"Here, here!" Lorna grabbed their wine glasses and handed them to Sophie and Heather. "To the love of Edwin and the downfall of Tottenstinker!"

"Here's to love and riches and fairytale endings," said Heather.

Sophie smiled. "Here's to me getting everything I deserve."

# Chapter Fifteen

The day after the whole interview disaster Steven suggested we hire from within. He came up with a miscellaneous girl who worked in my supposed data entry department. Brittney proved to be a wonder for us. Almost at once, Steven's workload was halved and he happily found himself with some free time. As much of a hard-worker as Steven, Brittney managed to complete many of the tasks and reports before the weekend. The arrangement seemed to make everyone happy.

Edwin and Sophie continued to pretend that they were being sneaky behind my back. Author forced me in a position to ignore what was happening to my face. Edwin, though, continued to complain to my face anytime I met up with Bob. I was an embarrassment to Edwin, but his taking Sophie to an exclusive premier was just business.

Bob and I continued to meet up at the park. It was through him that I learned that Sophie moved out of their little apartment and in with Edwin. Bob was trying to better himself now that Sophie was out of the picture. For as long as Author forgot about him, he managed to hold down a job as a mechanic and went to the gym. But, as soon as Author needed him for a scene, all his hard work faded for that moment. Luckily, Bob's boss understood and continued to rehire him.

Wednesday, in the second week of June, Edwin and Sophie reluctantly dragged me along for ring shopping and registry work. The jewelry store was first. While Sophie and Edwin cooed over the various jewelry displays, I marched right up to the wedding counter and started browsing. I wanted to find a band that would complement the marquis-cut diamond Edwin gave me so long ago. I was a bit disappointed to find that gold was not a prominent metal for wedding jewelry. Almost everything was either silver or platinum. After searching and trying on the few gold bands they had, I finally found one I liked. It was plain with a V-notch so it sat comfortably against my diamond with identical black diamonds on either side. It complimented my ring perfectly.

"Edwin? Come and look at this one. I think it might be the ring."

I turned to wave Edwin over. He was currently hooking a large necklace on Sophie. It was as thick as a belt with huge pink and clear diamonds set to look like flowers. It flowed over her slender neck and settled heavily on her abundant chest.

"Oh, Edwin, I think it looks marvelous," Sophie gushed. "But where would I ever wear something so grand?"

"I'm sure I can think of a few places," Edwin said. He bent and whispered in her ear, causing Sophie to blush a bright pink.

I cleared my throat. "If you are done playing dress-up with the jewelry, I have a ring I want you to look at, Edwin."

Edwin groaned and came over to see what I found. I showed him the ring, and he frowned. "Of course, Verucca, you'd pick the most expensive ring of the bunch."

"It's cheaper than the platinum version," I said. "Also, it has to work with the engagement ring. The only other option is to get a band and wear the engagement ring on the other hand."

Edwin grumbled. He finally picked up a plain gold band

that was only worth fifty dollars. The small band got lost under my engagement ring.

"There, that will do," Edwin said.

I shrugged. "As long as you don't mind my wearing the engagement ring on the other hand, I can live with this."

"You always make things so hard, Verucca. Just wear it like it's supposed to be worn and quit complaining."

Since I had a feeling it wouldn't matter what hand I wore my engagement ring by the time the book ended, I pretended to agree with him. "Oh, look, Edwin. There's a matching band for you." I pointed out the manlier version of the gold band.

"That's not Edwin's style at all," Sophie said. She pointed to a platinum band encircled with diamonds. "That's more his style."

"Call me old fashioned, but shouldn't the wedding bands match," I said.

Sophie twittered. "Silly. They don't have to match."

"This is just perfect for me," Edwin said.

"Edwin, dear," Sophie whined. She held up another gaudy necklace, this one a waterfall of sapphires and diamonds. "Wouldn't this look so beautiful on me?"

Before Edwin could answer, I said, "No, it wouldn't." I saw Edwin start to become red with anger and quickly picked up a simple tanzanite heart on a silver chain. "This is more you."

Edwin glared at me as he took the tanzanite heart from me. "Yes, actually I agree. See, Sophie, you are so gorgeous that you don't need all those gems around your neck. Something like this will let your inner beauty shine."

Sophie seemed mollified over that explanation. We left the store with our bands ordered and Sophie dragged us through the most high-end stores for our wedding registry. None of my suggestions made it on the list, and I was sickened to know that whatever home I should pretend would be mine after the wedding, would now consist of primarily pink everything.

A bit depressed, and not at all surprised, over how the shopping progressed, I went home. Steven was waiting for me, a huge grin on his face. I took one look at his outfit and couldn't help smiling myself. The top half of him looked like he was going to a gym with a sweat band pushing back his blond hair and a dark maroon tank top, while the bottom half of him looked more clubbing in a patch-work of dark leather jogging pants and boots.

"Now, Steven, you know I'm not that kind of girl."

"Never mind that. I got it!" He waved a thick stack of papers; the manuscript for our Story.

"*Planning His Pleasure*? I have no hopes with a title like that," I said.

"It's unfinished, mind you," Steven said. "I can only get what is written thus far. I think it covers up to today. Sorry, no cheats at the future."

I quickly thumbed through the manuscript. Surprisingly, the abuse heaped upon me was not as blatant in the book. Most of the action was seen through Edwin's or Sophie's eyes, and they barely gave me a second thought. All those times I paid for dinner while they crept out were not seen. Instead, Author followed them and my punishment was not revealed unless I talked with Edwin.

"Good gracious," I muttered. "She certainly jumped into bed with him fast. Her first few chapters are of how she's saving herself for marriage, won't let Bob see her in her nightgown, never been truly kissed, but the second she sees Edwin, she's in love. And they have sex for the first time after I left Shirley's office. So much for waiting for marriage."

"Yeah, I've seen that happen a lot before," Steven said. "Heroines like her are all like, 'I'm a twenty-six year old virgin and I'm going to wait for my Mr. Right, but I just met you and you're handsome and rich, so let's have sex'. And then the disco lights come on and she pulls out a whip."

"Pretty much how it happened," I said. "Except it seems more fairy-lights and really bad writing."

"How bad?"

I thumbed through the book and gave a shriek of laughter. "This bad," I said before dramatically reading, "And then, Edwin reared up and plunged his mighty man carrot into her heavenly lady gardens."

Steven patted me on the arm. "Just keep telling yourself it's almost over. We're in June. We have six months until the wedding. You're halfway there."

"I just want this to be over."

The next day, I found a surprise at the office. A huge bouquet of red roses waited for me on my desk, along with a jewelry box from the store Sophie took us to the other day. Curious, I opened the box and discovered a lovely garnet necklace and matching earrings. The card attached to the gifts read, "For yesterday. I'm sorry for the unpleasantness. Edwin"

"Maybe we were wrong and this is a turning point," Steven said.

"Maybe."

At the end of the day, I left my office a little early and made my way to Edwin's business. Sweeping by the receptionist, I opened the doors to his office. Edwin sat there, barely glancing up at me as he concentrated on the stack of papers in front of him.

"What do you want, Verucca?"

"I wanted to thank you," I said. "After everything we've been through, this was really thoughtful. I wanted to thank you in person instead of just calling you up."

"Thank me for what?"

I touched the necklace around my neck. "For this. And the flowers. Really, Edwin, they're perfect."

This time, he looked up. "What?" He stood and walked over to me. When he saw the jewelry, he frowned.

"I didn't send that to you."

"Yes, you did. The card said you were sorry for yesterday. It was signed by you."

Edwin shook his head. "No. It wasn't supposed to go to you. I bought that for Sophie."

I felt a coldness wash over me. "And why are you buying the wedding planner flowers and jewelry?"

"To thank her for all her hard work," Edwin said. "And for putting up with all your snide remarks and hateful comments. She's a real trooper."

I wanted to rip the necklace off and throw it in his face. "Why would you send her flowers and jewelry? You do realize her wedding ideas have us going over budget by three hundred percent? You don't reward someone for that!"

"It's your fault if we go over budget. You're the one who set it; you're the one who should keep it."

I waited to feel guidance from Author. It was then I realized that this was not a scene. Author was somewhere else at the moment. Edwin bought these gifts on his own.

Angered, I said, "We only have six more months, Edwin. Less if Author fast forwards a month here and there. I don't suppose it's asking too much for you and Sophie to not be so obvious in your affair? Your obliquity conduct thus far has really pushed my good nature to the limits. I may have to endure it while you cosset to her for Author's sake, but it would be nice if you didn't shove it in my face every chance you got!"

"Maybe it hasn't occurred to you, Verucca, but you're the villain in the Story. I don't have to do anything for you."

"It has occurred to me. I'm well aware of the fact that I am the Other Woman, the obstacle for you and Sophie to climb over. However, all good Characters are multi-faceted, and you have not tried to see any other side of me. I get that you want Sophie, and everyone knows that the book will end with the two of you together. Trust me, you two deserve each other. Unless driven by Author, I don't plan to stand in your way. All I ask is that you respect me enough to not flaunt your affair on your own time."

"I happen to truly love Sophie. When the Story ends, we plan on meeting up and marrying in Outer World." He sneered at me. "I hope you don't harbor any delusions that I might suddenly love you."

"Not a chance. You're not my type." I turned to leave, but his words stopped me.

"Give me back the jewelry. It wasn't meant for you and you know it."

Looking at him, I smiled. "No. I think I'll keep it. If Author wants Sophie to have them, she'll poof them to Sophie. Otherwise, they were given to me and, thus, will stay with me."

"Sophie was right about you! You are the worst person. You haven't changed since high school. This is the punishment you deserve for hurting poor Sophie."

"That's back story!" I held my arms out. "Author isn't here right now, Edwin. Who I am in the Story means nothing. Sophie wouldn't know me in Outer World, so our back story doesn't mean a thing. You wanting to punish me for back story is sad." And warranted therapy. If I knew who Edwin and Sophie were in Outer World, I'd alert the authorities that they were getting too far into their parts. It was a risk we Characters ran, but mostly manifested in series. A little stand-alone Story like this shouldn't have sucked him in this fast.

"It always means something. Author made you the villain because you're evil. That's all you'll ever be."

I rolled my eyes and left. His comment on my back story mattering stuck with me. Maybe I should look into Verucca Tottenstinker before she became the owner of Tabby Pops? If my back story collided with Sophie's, I should learn all I could before Author decided to surprise me.

# Chapter Sixteen

The flower incident happened on a Thursday. I decided that I would travel to my hometown to discover more of my past and leave that weekend. All day Friday, I prepared myself for an absence of work and instructed Steven on what to do in various emergencies. In the end, the go-to decision would be to call me.

I told Edwin I wanted to travel home to find my old prom dress and turn it into silk roses for the toss bouquet. He snorted and commented that I probably wouldn't find it.

Before I left, I got a call from Bambi. She sent me pictures of what the bridesmaids' dresses were to look like, and I immediately called Sophie to complain.

"They are hideous!" Sophie decided at some point in time that the pink and cream wedding should also be a fairytale wedding. So, the bridesmaids all got dresses that not even an ugly stepsister would wear. The top layer of the Renaissance Fair rip-off was pink with puffy shoulder pads and the top skirt gathered around knee-height to show the cream skirt beneath. The built-in bodice was little more than decoration.

"Oh, they look fine," Sophie said. "You do know the whole point of bridesmaids are, right?"

"In the ancient days, they were used as decoys so that if a spurned lover or enemy of the family tried to kidnap the bride, there was a chance he'd grab the wrong person. Now they are just to show off the friends of the bride."

Sophie twittered. "No, silly. Bridesmaids exist to make the bride look good. And let's be honest, trying to make you look good is nearly impossible."

"So you deliberately gave my bridesmaids hideous dresses? I would rather they wore something more fitting for the wedding and risk them outshining me, than force them to wear something so ugly and make them miserable."

"They will still outshine you. Even dressed like that."

I gnashed my teeth. "We will talk further when I get back."

"Going on a trip?" Now she sounded interested. Probably plotting more meetings with Edwin.

"It's no secret. I'm going home. I wanted to see if I could get my hands on my prom dress. Until I get back, there is to be no further plans on the wedding. I mean it, Sophie! I am not there to sign anything, and I will press charges if my name is signed on any documents. I'm also cutting off all my credit cards that I know you've used."

Sophie sniffled and I heard her cry out, "She's threatening to fire me again! Oh, Edwin, all I was doing was trying to help her out by downplaying her bridesmaids."

Edwin's voice came over the phone. "Verucca! Can't you be nice for one day?"

"Gee, the two of you are together. Why am I not surprised? You'd better be careful, Edwin, or not even Author can shield your infidelities from the Reader."

I hung up and ignored my phone for the entire trip to my home town. As I drove, I tried to picture my past. I only got a few fragments here and there, the memory of feeling bittersweet, and a name, Juliette, ran through my mind. Whenever I tried to clasp on to that name, I felt like crying.

I possessed a house in my hometown, left to me when my parents died. For some reason, Author never had me sell the house. I was rather used to not having parents, as many of my

Characters suffered the "no parent back story." I had real parents waiting for me in Outer World, and that was all that mattered to me.

I was enormously surprised to find my hometown existed. I almost expected to find myself in an empty field, where I would stay until my trip was up. What I found was a bustling little town with a white steeple church, colorful storefronts, charming houses, and a railway track that split the left side of the town into the haves and the have-nots.

I found my home on the wrong side of the tracks and quickly went in. I was not sure of my reception in town, being the Story's villain. My childhood home was surprisingly free of dust and looked extraordinarily well-cared for. I slowly made my way up to my old bedroom. Standing in the doorway, I stared at the room, letting foreign memories flood over me.

I hated the navy blue bedspread my mom bought me. I wanted a Power Princess one, but it was too much money.

My high school books still sat on my desk, wrapped in paper bags and doodles all over them. If I looked, I knew I'd find my childhood dreams of being "Mrs. Eric Peters" all over the front.

A small collection of porcelain cats sat on the windowsill. I bought each chipped and smudged piece at garage sales with my allowance money.

Sitting on the bed were two fashion dolls. One had clay molded over the body to make the normally ultra-thin doll fat, while the other one resembled me. I picked up the dolls and smiled.

*Now they look like us, Juliette.*

I gasped and turned, expecting to see the person who just

spoke. No one stood there and it took me far longer than I'd ever admit to realize that was a memory.

I decided to get something to eat after my long journey. I washed up and headed out into town. There wasn't much to choose from, just the stereotypical greasy spoon on this side of the tracks, and more upscale diner on the other side. I found myself heading to the greasy spoon, memories of eating there as a child filled me.

It looked the same. The overweight woman behind the counter smoked a cigar, her fleshy, tattooed arms leaning against the counter and her wiry black hair pulled back in a bun. Her name was Agnes, and I remembered that she was only gruff because she cared.

When Agnes saw, she slapped the counter, causing all the other wrong-side of the track patrons to quiet down. "Why, Verucca Tottenstinker! Our prodigal daughter has returned." She moved quicker than I would have thought and caught me in a huge bear hug.

"Hello Agnes. I'm only visiting for a few days."

"Shoot, honey, we were waiting for you. You stayed away too long." Agnes ushered me over to a seat at the counter. I easily recognized several of the people in the little restaurant. There was Big Larry, a truck driver and single father. His son graduated with me. Over to my right were the Wolfe twins, mechanics who were always covered in grease and oil, and looked as if they belonged behind bars. The school's janitor was there, looking tired from a night of hard work. All blue-collar workers who lived in little homes and drove cars that were held together with spit and a prayer.

"I'm getting married in December," I said. "I came back to find some things from home to include in the wedding."

Agnes snorted. "That's the reason in the Story, honey. Author ain't here. What really brings you out this way?"

I looked around and found myself met with friendly eyes. I recognized a few from Outer World. They attended regular meetings of *Every Time Villains*. Feeling at home, I said, "I need to find out about my past. It keeps coming up, even outside of the storyline. Something happened here, and I know it's a huge part of the Story. However, Author has not granted me the memory of it, so I feel weaponless."

Big Larry nodded. "Yeah, we figured that might be the reason. Not going to be a happy marriage."

"Not going to be a marriage at all," I said. "I've faced facts. I may get as far as the altar, but in the end, it's going to be Edwin and Sophie."

One of the Wolfe brothers spat on the floor, causing Agnes to reach across the counter and smack the top of his head. Looking sheepish, he said, "We don't speak of her here. As we are your background story, we know what you're here to seek."

"Care to fill me in?"

"Naw. I think you should discover it on your own. More fun that way."

The cook, a burly man named Cookie, came out of the kitchen with a plate of fries so fresh the grease was still sizzling and a burger the size of my head. He placed it in front of me and shuffled back off to the kitchen. My memories told me that was a huge deal for him because he never came out of the kitchen.

"Know what, honey?" Agnes said. "I'll give you a clue on where to start looking. You might get a few ideas at your house, but the house behind yours holds the answer. If I were you, I'd start my search there first thing in the morning."

I finished my burger and caught up with the people I recognized. They enjoyed playing background characters, and this was an easy stint. After I found my answers and left, they'd all go home. There was no antagonist here to ruin the good time.

# Chapter Seventeen

The next morning, I went to check the house behind me. While my house was a simple single story home that resembled a large trailer, this one was smaller with dirt and cobwebs everywhere. Broken toys littered the yard and a beat up old truck sat forlornly on cement blocks. I doubted anyone still lived there, but I was told to check it out.

As I walked up, I could see a curtain flutter. Someone was inside, watching me. Hesitantly, I knocked on the front door. The dark interior was silent, and I wondered if the movement was a trick of the mind. I knocked a second time and listened.

Silence.

I took a step back, ready to leave, when the door opened. The person standing in the doorway was a teenager, a chubby girl with an overabundance of freckles and curly blonde hair. Her little stub nose was turned up and the flesh of her cheeks pushed up so much when she smiled that her blue eyes almost vanished behind the mounds.

*"Verucca! Hey, glad you could make it. I just know I'm going to fail trigonometry without you. Mom has some snacks on the table for us."*

I reached out to her. "Juliette?"

The teenager's form wavered and was replaced by an elderly woman. She had the same chubby frame and freckles as the teen, but her blonde hair was now gray with white streaks. She wore a tattered robe and bunny slippers. In an instant, I knew she was the teen's mom.

"I knew you'd be back," the woman said. She smiled and

pulled me into a hug. "It's not in your nature to stay away for long."

"I'm here to remember," I said. "Something happened here that is going to affect the Story, something between myself and Sophie Winslow."

"Prom night. I remember all of it. You were best friends with my little Juliette. The two of you were inseparable from the day you pushed Sophie into the mud for pushing my daughter. That was your first day of Kindergarten."

I entered the small home, which appeared bigger on the inside. There was the battered old TV that Juliette and I used to watch black and white movies on, and there was the kitchen where we did our homework together. I remembered now, sitting at that table while Juliette's mom cut my hair after we found someone stuck gum in it.

My eyes were drawn to an urn sitting on the counter. Someone painted frolicking pixies on the somber white surface.

"Prom was her last happy memory," Juliette's mom said. "You made that possible, Verucca. She was born with a heart defect. Her medicine made it impossible for her to lose weight, and her weight added to her problems. All throughout your schooling, you two were bullied if found alone. Some of the neighborhood boys would hang out with the two of you to protect you, but those three bullies always found you. Juliette suffered years of name calling, having her possessions stolen, and being shoved into trash cans. The worst came before prom, when you found her crying behind the school. Do you remember that? It's when you decided to give her one night of happiness."

I did remember. Juliette and I always walked home

together, but I managed to snag detention that day. I couldn't remember why. I thought Juliette would get a ride home with one of the boys from our neighborhood and be safe. She decided to wait for me instead, and was cornered by Sophie, Heather, and Lorna. When I left school, I nearly passed Juliette since I assumed she was gone.

It was Juliette's whimpers of pain that alerted me of her hiding place. Curled up behind the large trash bins, she was a bloody mess. The terrorizing trio did a number on her.

In the present, I looked over at Juliette's urn. "It was more than just the bullies that day. I hadn't seen her all day long. She wasn't there at the beginning of school and I never thought she'd wait at the end." I frowned, trying to grasp the memories. "There was something else that was wrong that day."

Her mom nodded. "We went to the doctor."

*"Juliette! Geez, what did they do to you? Come on, let's get you home."*

*"I'm okay. Really."*

*"No you're not! I thought you were going home. Why didn't you leave with Lonnie and Otis? They would have protected you."*

*"I had to talk to you."*

*"You could have talked to me at home. Come on, upsie-daisy."*

*"Verucca, I am getting the operation. The doctor said they'll do it, but it can be dangerous."*

*"When?"*

*"A week after prom. Who knows, I might graduate from my hospital room."*

*"How dangerous is the operation?"*

*"Incredibly dangerous. I overheard the doctor tell mom that I only have a twenty percent chance of surviving because of my*

*weakened state, but it's better than nothing.*"

Juliette's mom was watching me. "You remember?"

"She was so scared to have that operation," I said. "She tried to be brave, but I knew it scared her. She said something about not wanting to die and not having any happy memories of school. I wanted to change that."

"You did. You went on a private crusade in that school and convinced enough of the student body to vote for her to be prom queen." Juliette's mom chuckled. "You dragged her to prom with your entourage of boys from the wrong side of the tracks. She won and got to dance with the star quarterback."

"And Sophie Winslow was not pleased with that. Wasn't she dating the star quarterback?"

It all came back to me. Juliette, wearing a pink and cream ruffled dress, dancing with a boy wearing a crown. Several other students whose faces blended into the unknown cheered for them, the spotlight following just them. Off to the side were Sophie and her friends, angry at what they were witnessing.

*"You did this Tottenstinker! You ruined my prom!"*

Juliette's mom and I spoke for hours about the past. Though Author was nowhere to be found, I felt the compulsion to remain in character. This was important to my story. I needed to learn all I could.

That night, I called Steven to tell him what I discovered. "I don't get it," I said. "I'm supposed to be this antagonist who ruined Sophie's life in the past and is now trapping the love of her life in a sham of a marriage. Yet, when the past is investigated, it's revealed that I did a good thing and haven't touched Sophie until we met in the Story. If anything, I have a

Hero's Past. Why would Author give me that back story if it doesn't matter?"

"Maybe it's not Author," he said. "I mean, Author seems to be more interested in pointing out how you're the villain, so what purpose would it serve to give you a good back story? If it were Author, don't you think you'd be the evil bully in the school who blackmailed and threatened the kids to make you prom queen? Or, let Sophie win and dump pig's blood on her? You know, something evil?"

"If my back story doesn't come from Author, then where would it come from? Author creates all."

"The Plot."

I groaned. "Oh, Steven, not you, too."

"Hear me out, Verucca. We all know Author comes up with the Plot, right? But we also know there have been cases in which the Plot and Author don't agree. That's where we get things like plot holes and consistency issues. Like this one. Author has one plan for you, and something else obviously has another. So, why not the Plot?"

"Steven, only crackpots believe in the Living Plot. It's a fairytale we tell ourselves when we are stuck in a Story that doesn't go our way, a misplaced faith that something else will save us from Author and give us a happy ending. There is no Living Plot."

"Just keep an open mind, Verucca. That's all I ask."

I rolled my eyes, knowing he couldn't see that over the phone. "Fine, I'll keep an open mind," I lied. "Now, what's going on back home?"

"Not much yet. Just Edwin and Sophie in their first official public appearance. You weren't gone an hour before they came out to say they were dating."

"They do remember he's still engaged to me?"

"Do you think it matters?"

I sighed. "Of course not. Assuming we're wrong and the Story goes beyond the wedding, they will continue to see each other. It won't matter to them what is proper, as long as they get what they want."

I didn't tell Steven, but in that moment, I felt like I was in parallel Stories. In one, I was engaged to Edwin and I had the Hero's Past and things would end happily. In the other, I was the villain and he would end up with Sophie because Sophie needed to win.

I wished I knew which Story would win.

# Chapter Eighteen

I stayed in my hometown for two weeks, learning all that I could about myself and Sophie. The more I learned, the more confused I became. I was not the evil villain I was portrayed. One of my favorite charities helped supply schools like mine with funding for music and art programs, provided computers and books to those who couldn't afford any, and helped start a work-mentor program for students to shadow those in their chosen field to better understand that field for when they graduated. I provided a scholarship to my school for students to have the chance to go to college.

How could I be the villain? All these things were tinged with some evil intent, but they were noble ideals.

I made one stop on my way back to the city. At a tiny cemetery just outside of my hometown, I visited Juliette's grave. A whole lifetime filled me, and I knelt by the tombstone and cried. All villains had a past, but this was the first time I really got to learn about mine. Maybe Steven was right. Maybe, all of my past was not Author's doing. I had not felt Author at all in my visit. Only a peek at the manuscript would tell me what I needed to know, but now, I was scared at what I would find.

What if Author found out what I did and punished me for it?

"Don't worry, Juliette," I whispered. "I won't let Sophie get away with this. Your happy memory should not be the plot device for her revenge."

"Oh, don't do that. You're better than that, Verucca."

I turned to see Juliette standing behind me. She was dressed in her prom gown, and looked happy.

"How? How are you here?"

She shrugged. "I was needed, so I got pulled in. I came to give you an important message."

"What message?"

"Don't seek revenge. You're better than that. No matter how awful any of your Stories ended, you always looked to forgive. No matter what terrible things you were forced to do, you tried to heal. Just because this Author wants you to be the villain, don't be consumed by it. You are who you have always been, and should do what you always do. Who cares if Sophie and Edwin win in this Story as long as you continue to be true to yourself?"

"All I wanted was a Happily Ever After," I said. "I know I won't get that now, but it doesn't stop me from wanting it."

"There is more than one Happily Ever After. The one you want is not the one for you. Find out what the right Happily Ever After is for you, and you will flourish."

By the time I got back to Faycrest, summer was underway. The heat radiated off the sidewalks and the winter chill of the start of the Story was but a distant memory. A new season, another scene closer to the end, and all I wanted to do was confront Sophie and Edwin. While I was gone, they became the darlings of the city. A perfect pair.

On Juliette's suggestion, I focused my efforts on myself. I tried harder to find out about this blackmail accusation. I joined a yoga group to deal with my stress. I took a more active role in the Cat Camp, protecting it against Heather. I stopped caring that Sophie was really planning her own wedding with my money. It wasn't like I'd get to keep any of it when I left the Story. I stopped caring that she and Edwin were seeing each other behind my back. I had long decided that Edwin was not the man for me. When Author was pulling the strings, I let her. I did what I always did in a Story, and tried to make the best of things.

I started taking lunches with Bob, and ignoring Lorna's lies in the paper the following day. We discussed endings and the path of the character. Sometimes, we discussed Edwin and Sophie.

"I just don't think she understands the situation," Bob said one afternoon. We were having lunch at a cute family cafe, letting the happy shrieks of children drown out our conversation. "Believe me, I've tried talking to her, but it goes in one ear and out the other. She still insists she's only helping him with the wedding. Not even showing her the articles have helped."

"Yeah, Edwin is the same way. Even if I don't bring up him and Sophie, he manages to find some way to talk about it. If I didn't know better, I'd say he was taunting me."

Bob, like myself, decided to better himself. When Author permitted it, he shaved and wore nicer clothes. He cut his hair and started going to the gym. Every time I saw him, I had a strange feeling I knew him from somewhere. He confided he normally played heroes, but I couldn't put my finger on it. Maybe I saw him outside a meeting?

"Sophie never comes home anymore. She's moved all of her stuff out, but I doubt she moved them into Edwin's apartment. I think she sold them for extra cash. I have to go out to the apartment every once in a while to beg for her to come back, or threaten her."

"You'd think Author would let us go. We really don't

~ 147 ~

serve a purpose anymore. Sophie and Edwin are together." I poked at my pasta for a moment. "Well, you serve no purpose any more. I'm still needed since it's my money paying for the wedding. I need to stick around long enough to make all the payments before Author gets rid of me."

"Why not just have Edwin pay for all of it?"

I shrugged. "Must be more satisfying to have the enemy pay for the wedding?"

We sat there in silence for a bit. Bob enjoyed his burger and I ate half my pasta. We agreed on pie for dessert. At the moment, Author was paying attention to Edwin and Sophie at some charity lunch that Edwin was supposed to take me before he canceled.

"I feel more like a villain," I confessed. "I want Sophie and Edwin to break up. I want them to feel the pain of having everything taken away. Even though I know it won't last, I want them to feel that."

"I want them to pay, too," Bob said. He took a bite of his pie. "It's humiliating that everyone knows Sophie is cheating on me, and I'm not allowed to leave her."

"You'll get your chance by the end. How else will she and Edwin get their Happily Ever After?"

"The ending can't come soon enough."

That night, I got a call from Edwin. He yelled at me for having lunch with Bob. When I pointed out he had lunch with Sophie, he told me it was apples and oranges.

"She and I discussed the wedding, Verucca. It's not what your sick mind is making it out to be."

"Pot and kettle, Edwin. Bob and I are merely friends, discussing philosophies about life. If you can have lunch with Sophie, I can have lunch with Bob. Much less happens between us than with you two."

The next day was our meeting with the priest of the Cathedral. What changed Author's mind about us meeting with him, I wasn't sure. I went prepared. No matter what, I would handle this as a woman who knew her fiancé was cheating. I may be forced to continue with this wedding farce, and I may still be dancing to Author's tune, but I was not going to make the way easy for Edwin and Sophie.

The priest, a stereotypical old man with little hair on his head and bushy eyebrows, who stooped over as if the weight of the world were on his frail shoulders, greeted us and ushered us to his office. He wanted to know why we picked this Cathedral and what did we hope to gain from our wedding. Edwin answered for both of us, and everything was peppered with the phrases, "Sophie said" and "Sophie believes".

"I thought your name was Verucca," the priest said when Edwin finally paused for breath.

"Sophie Winslow is the wedding planner's assistant who is *assisting* us with the wedding," I said. My fingers twitched to make air quotes around "assisting", but I think he understood.

"And what are your plans?" the priest asked.

"Verucca agrees with me," Edwin said quickly. He shot me a look that said for me to keep my mouth shut. "Sophie is qualified and her wedding plans are the absolute best. She is the one who suggested we come here."

The priest frowned slightly. "Well, I am going to tell you what I always tell my parishioners before they can start wedding plans..."

"We aren't part of this church," Edwin said. "We just want to use the building."

"Why not use a building of your faith?"

"Because this is where Sophie believes our wedding should take place."

The priest looked over at me as Author started pushing harder on the scene. From the look in his eyes, I could tell he wanted to protest, but Author wouldn't allow it.

"Very well. For now, I want you both to get six months of couples counseling and purchase wedding insurance."

Edwin balked. "Couples counseling? Why would we need that?"

"I suggest everyone gets it. It will help you in the future. You may need it to iron out some little wrinkles in your current happiness."

"We are fine without it. And since it's something only for your parishioners, we decline." Edwin sat back and crossed his arms.

"What is wedding insurance?" I asked.

"It's to help protect your investments. On any vendor or venue you book, get insurance to help cover your assets. This way, if something happens beyond your control, you get your money back."

I thought about this. "Would it also ensure that whoever is named are the parties covered?"

"What do you mean, my child?"

"Well, if I sign up for the Cathedral for the wedding between myself and Edwin, then only if the wedding is between myself and Edwin it would go on. If, say for instance, it is between Edwin and Sophie, then the contract is null and void and the insurance reimburses me?"

Edwin scoffed in his seat, still looking like a petulant child. "What about if it's between Bob and yourself? Would I get the money?"

"Only what you put into the wedding," the priest said. "If, for example, Ms. Tottenstinker put in one hundred percent of the costs and was pushed out of the wedding for another bride, she would get one hundred percent back. Now, if she put one hundred percent in, and you were pushed aside for another groom, she would not get a penny back, but neither would you. You put nothing in." The priest leaned back and shrugged. "Though, it doesn't cover change of heart, so this is all hypothetical. Wedding insurance is for the practical mishaps that can happen at a wedding: venue snowed in, lost luggage, missing limos, liquor licenses, and the like."

"But, there is some kind of wedding clause that states, if you are to perform the wedding between myself and Edwin, it can only be between myself and Edwin?"

"Well, yes. To charge you for someone else's wedding is just immoral."

I smiled. "Thank you. That puts my mind at ease."

The priest leaned forward as we felt the grip of Author lessen. "I don't suppose the two of you ever thought of, I don't know, not getting married?"

"Yes. All the time," said Edwin.

# Chapter Nineteen

The Friday after our meeting with the priest, I found the infamous contract. I was surprised to find that it had been in my apartment the whole time. Tucked away in the inglenook, between two large books, it was nothing more than three pages. Far thinner than what I was expecting, considering I was supposed to be some kind of manipulative contract-writing genius who wove a twisted web and ensnared the innocent Edwin in a tangled labyrinth of double entendre of witty words. The contract was, surprisingly, straight forward.

And completely illegal.

According to the contract, around the same point in time we started dating, Edwin borrowed a million dollars from me. The reason was never stated, and I did some research in my many diaries and appointment books to no avail. This made no sense. Not only would I have written the reason, but I could see no reason for Edwin to need to borrow money from me. He was a successful business man who could buy me out a hundred times over, and if he needed money, he would have gone to a bank. The contract stated that he was to pay me back in full by one year's time, or start paying interest. Oddly, I did have a clause stating that if we became engaged and married, the debt would be forgiven upon signing the marriage certificate.

"So, instead of paying me back when it was interest free, he proposed," I mused. The interest didn't start until New Year's Day, which he now didn't have to worry about as long as we were together.

I looked over the interest, and nearly doubled over laughing. It was beyond illegal. Should we break up, he was expected to pay me back the original one million plus an interest of twenty-five percent per week. Anyone with half a brain would see that this contract was null and void based solely on the idiotic writing.

I kept the contract with me after that. I didn't tell Steven I found it, worried that Author might overhear. Instead, I started drafting a new contract that would make this one null and void once I got Edwin to sign. A more reasonable contract where he only owed me the original one million, no interest, and could do a payment plan for fifteen years. A man as rich as he should find that reasonable.

That next Wednesday was a spa retreat with my bridesmaids. With the wedding now only five months away, the girls said they wanted to treat me to some relaxation before the real stress began. We drove out to Tranquility Spa and Gardens for a day of massages and pampering. We scheduled with an aromatic massage, make overs, and a milk bath.

The aromatic massage lifted all the stress from me, and I already felt like a new woman. Feeling refreshed, the five of us went to get our make overs. Bambi wanted a shorter hairstyle while Amanda decided to dye her hair bright fire engine red. Virginia wanted only a trim, but also opted to have a manicure and pedicure. Latona said she wanted curls and Rosie wanted streaks of gold and black.

"And what about you, ma'am," the hairstylist asked. "What can we do for you today?"

"Just a trim and shape up," I said.

"Come on, Verucca! Do something fun," Bambi said.

"Live a little," urged Rosie.

"No. I don't want Edwin to freak out. Let's just stay safe."

Latona rolled her eyes. "Girl, forget him. Today is about you. Do you really want to look like the old witch in the gingerbread house? Get some body in your hair."

I thought it over. "Well, I guess we can try to put some highlights in. What do you suggest?" I looked at the stylist.

She frowned, running her fingers through my thin hair. She hummed a bit, tilting my head from side to side. "I can do that, I guess."

"Okay. Some highlights it is."

The hairstylist sniffed. "Very well. We must shampoo you first and then bleach your hair. Otherwise, the highlights won't show up. Follow me." The six of us headed to the back sinks. My bridesmaids all got their own stylists while I retained the woman with whom we discussed our plans.

"Oh, this feels like heaven," Amanda said with a sigh. I agreed. The pampering of the warm water and massage felt so wonderful. I could almost fall asleep in the chair. Afterward, she led me to the chair and got started on my hair. In this spa, they kept the chair turned away from the mirror. The reveal of the new you was a production, and even trim warranted a grand reveal.

"Okay, now we will reveal the new you." The stylist twirled me around so I could see myself for the first time. Once I laid eyes upon my visage, my mouth fell open. The person in the mirror couldn't be me.

"My hair is green!" My voice came out in a squeak. My hair was now snot-green, still hanging in limp strands. This was not what I expected.

"Yes, ma'am. I noticed."

"How could this happen?"

She shrugged, as if she couldn't care less. "Your hair changed after the shampoo treatment. Maybe you had a reaction? If you only use cheap shampoo at home, your hair can go into shock when we use our high-end, elite brands."

"There is no such thing as hair shock! And if you saw that the shampoo damaged my hair, why didn't you say anything?"

"Lower your voice, Ms. Tottenstinker. There is no reason to be upset."

"My hair is green! Fix it!"

"What is going on here?" A short man waddled over to us. He was finely dressed and his name tag read, 'Jameson, Manager'.

"My hair is green," I said. "Your stylist knew about it and didn't say anything. I should have been told something happened with my hair as soon as she noticed it."

Jameson critically eyed my hair. "Yes, an unfortunate shade, but we can't control what your dye job does to your hair."

"I didn't get a dye job," I said. "I got a shampoo and I was supposed to get it trimmed to show some body. No hair dye at all!"

"Her hair went into shock," the stylist explained. "She should stop using such cheap shampoo."

The manager nodded. "Problem solved."

"Problem not solved. My hair is green. Fix it!"

Jameson frowned. "There is no need to get testy, ma'am. This is all your fault."

"Then dye my hair back to black. Fix it. I have meetings tomorrow and a business to run. I can't go around with green hair."

"There is nothing we can do. Your hair is naturally damaged. If I dye it, it will become brittle and fall out," the stylist said. "This is all your fault."

"You turned my hair green." I tried to keep my voice steady, but I felt myself shaking. "A proper business would seek a way to fix the problem and keep their client happy. A bad company would do nothing. Which are you?"

"Ma'am, I won't have you bad mouth my resort," Jameson said. "Please leave."

"I demand you rectify this situation! I am not pleased with my appointment. What ever happened to keeping the customer happy?"

"We do not have to keep you happy. Get out of my spa and never return."

"Refund my money and I will."

"No. You got your hair styled, so you must pay for services rendered."

"What about my afternoon appointments? I will not be there, thus I shouldn't have to pay for services not rendered."

"Ma'am, we don't refund if you cancel less than twenty-four hours. We cannot refund any of your money."

My eye twitched as I stared down at Jameson. "But, legally, I am not canceling. You are forcing me to leave, so I should get my money back."

"Leave, or I'm calling security!"

I knew I'd get nowhere. On my way out, I was forced to settle my bill. My bridesmaids pretended to not know me so they could stay. To add insult to injury, when I got my total, I found out I was paying for the whole resort anyway. So much for my bridesmaids treating me. I was expecting to pay at least my way, but I ended up paying for them to enjoy the whole day.

I left, finding my car mysteriously waiting for me. On my way home, I called my lawyer and told him I wanted to sue the resort for their treatment of me and to get my money back for services not rendered to my enjoyment. He informed me that I would lose, but agreed to get the paperwork started.

I then called Steven. "I'll be waiting for you with wine and wigs," he said.

"Thank you," I said.

"I can't believe that anything this childish would happen. I mean, how can it show Sophie in a good light to pull such a juvenile prank?" Steven asked.

I thought it over. "I don't know. I should have known something was going on with how much attention Author was paying to that scene." I sighed, feeling my previous stress-free mood leave for good. "I honestly hoped that I was in an Ugly Duckling Story. That this would be my turning point. I guess this is the nail in my coffin."

"Yeah. Sorry, Verucca."

"Forget the wine and wigs," I said. "I'm going to need hard liqueur or chocolate. I'll be home after I confront Sophie."

"Why? Is Author demanding it?"

"No. But this is something I have to do." I turned the car in the direction of Sophie's upscale apartment. It was time to confront Sophie.

# Chapter Twenty

The apartment building where Sophie now lived was, naturally, painted pink. In a sea of boring gray office buildings and brick townhouses, the large baby-pink building really stood out. I pulled my car into the parking garage and found a visitor spot. The elevators in the garage were for residents only, and I walked out to the front.

I didn't have to wonder which apartment would be Sophie's. The penthouse would be the most expensive and beautiful place, thus that was where I headed. When I stepped out of the elevator, I found Sophie's door open and green handprints around the door frame. I shrugged, grateful that I would not have to find a way to break into the apartment.

I heard voices near the back and slowly crept toward them. Sophie, Heather, and Lorna were in the bathroom, the door partly closed to keep me from view. I could feel Author's presence, but I think my being there surprised her.

"This stuff is really permanent," Heather was saying, and I heard the sound of water running. "Man, it just won't come off! I'm going to be green forever."

"Just think," said Lorna, "if we can't get it off our hands, Tottenstinker won't ever get it out of her hair."

"This is perfect, you two. Now Tottenstinker will have to call off the wedding. There is no way she'll want to be seen in public with green hair," said Sophie.

"You should have heard her, Sophie," Heather said. She raised her voice in a bad, screechy imitation of my own. "You turned my hair green! I demand you rectify the situation! Blah

blah blah, I'm Tottenstinker and I'm so important!"

Lorna's own hateful imitation followed. "I want my money back. You can't do this to me." She laughed. "Sophie, she was in such a fit."

"She wouldn't believe it when they told her hair went into shock. Can you believe her arrogance?"

From where I stood, I rolled my eyes. Of course I didn't believe my hair went into shock. That was too stupid for words. Not to mention, it wasn't shock since they were washing the dye off their hands.

"I wish I could have seen the look on her ugly face," Sophie said. She opened the bathroom door and saw me.

"Wish granted," I said.

I saw the look of panic come over their faces. How much did I overhear? What did I know? How did I get in? Behind Sophie, Heather and Lorna furiously scrubbed their hands to get rid of the evidence.

Sophie's eyes flickered up to my snot-green hair. "Nice hairstyle, Tottenstinker. Now get out of my home."

I felt Author try to push me aside. Oh, no! We were having this scene. It could end up on the editor's floor for all I cared; I was going to speak my mind.

"I know everything," I said. "I know your friends dyed my hair. I know this penthouse belongs to Edwin as one of his many secret get-aways. I know you and Edwin had sexual relations. I've known all of this for a long time, Sophie. I've been as nice as I could be, praying that the two of you would come to your senses and do the right thing. I've even offered Edwin his freedom, but he said he wanted to continue our wedding plans. I am tired of tiptoeing around the two of you, pretending I don't see the looks and touches behind my back."

~ 159 ~

"I don't know what you're talking about, Tottenstinker," Sophie huffed. "I am just the wedding planner. Nothing is going on."

"No one believes that, Sophie. A wedding planner isn't rewarded with trips to Hollywood premiers, private yacht rides, or expensive penthouses. Those are things a lover gets."

"And yet, Edwin's never rewarded you with any of those things," Heather said. She smirked, shaking the water from her still slightly green hands. "Jealous."

"Hardly. I have ceased to care about the affections between Sophie and Edwin. Fine. As soon as I can break my engagement, I will. For some reason, Edwin refuses to let me go."

"You know why," Lorna said. "You're blackmailing him."

"Am I really? Makes one wonder what horrible skeleton Edwin must have in his closet that marriage to me is preferred to it being let out." I looked over at Sophie. "And, really Sophie, I've put up with your childish attempts to replace me in the past, but green hair? How juvenile. Did you honestly think that a change in hair color would cause me to stop the wedding? Or were you hoping Edwin would break up with me because of an unfortunate hairstyle?"

Sophie drew herself up to her full height. "Edwin would not be affected by anything as shallow as looks. He's the deepest man I've ever met."

"I've seen puddles in the desert deeper."

Lorna pulled Sophie behind her. "What makes you think any of us is responsible? Maybe your cheap shampoo caused your ugly, greasy hair to go into shock when it actually had contact with something of substance?"

"Oh, well, you mean besides the fact you just used the

same idiotic excuse the spa tried to sell me? For one, I heard you just now admitting to the dye job. Two, you both still have the dye on your hands. I caught you green-handed, as it were."

"All of this was discovered after you broke in," Lorna declared. "Fruit of the poisoned tree. Not admissible in court."

"Your door was wide open," I said. "I did not break in. What you have is a flaw in the design."

"You can stop acting so superior," Sophie scoffed. "I know all about you. You're only marrying Edwin for his money and because of his looks. If he were poor or looked like Bob, you wouldn't care."

"And, yet, ironically, I do care about Bob. He's a sweet man with plenty to offer. I'd take him over Edwin any day," I said.

"You're a cheater! Edwin deserves better than you!" Sophie acted as if she wanted to lunge from behind Lorna, but I knew better. She was a coward.

"My, my, isn't that the pot calling the kettle black. All of the city knows about your and Edwin's sexcapades. Lorna has been such a dear and printed each one in loving detail. With pictures. I have a whole file on Edwin's infidelity."

"You're an evil woman!" Sophie buried her head against Lorna's shoulder and cried.

Pushing forward, I decided to go for Personal Redemption. I had Author's attention, and I hoped that this much got through. "I went back to our hometown, Sophie. I talked to a lot of people who remembered us. What I discovered changes everything."

"What could you possibly have discovered," sneered Heather.

"That you were not the poor, abused heroine you pretend to be. You, Sophie Winslow, grew up in a wealthy upper-middle class family, went to prestigious summer camps, was in the top five of your class, graduated valedictorian, dated the star quarterback, and was head cheerleader. Heather and Lorna were always at your side. The only box you left unchecked was prom queen our senior year."

"Because you ruined my prom!"

"If you were the heroine, my actions should be your own! The girl who won, Juliette, was a poor girl who never had any luck in life. She died on the operating table a week after prom, while in surgery to try and repair her heart. That prom was her last happy memory, and you are selfishly rallying against it because you didn't get some stupid crown!"

"I was supposed to be prom queen!" Sophie stomped her foot, looking all the world like a petulant child. "You took it away from me. No one wanted me after that! I had to go to a crappy little college and then date Bob and accept measly little jobs. All because I wasn't prom queen!"

"I wasn't prom queen, yet I managed to make the best of it. I graduated beneath you, I lived in a run-down little house on the wrong side of the tracks, I was a nobody, yet I managed to make something of myself. Your accusations don't make sense, Sophie. A good college won't toss you out because you weren't prom queen. You just decided to let that one set back rule your life. And now, you're letting it become your excuse to steal what doesn't belong to you!"

"My life is finally turning around," Sophie said. She stepped in front of Lorna, ready to face me. "You're just jealous that Edwin loves me. We are going to get married and live the high life. He'll pamper me with his money. You,

Tottenstinker, will go back to being a dirty, ugly little nobody from the wrong side of the tracks with a pig for a best friend." She giggled. "Oopsie, my bad. The pig died, didn't she?"

"You really haven't changed, have you? You were a bully in school, and you're a bully now. You liked taking the easy way out, and Edwin is your ticket to everything you ever wanted." I pulled out a piece of paper from my pants pocket. It was a copy of our senior pictures, along with our personal quotes. I read, "Sophie Winslow says her wish is to be rich and famous and never have to work."

"That doesn't mean anything!"

"And here you are, sneaking around with a man you know is engaged. A rich man, I might add, who spends his money on you all the time. Marrying him will get you what you've always wanted; yachts, parties, trips around the world, designer clothes, and servants."

"What about you?" sneered Lorna. "You get the same thing."

"No, I don't. I have my own money to buy yachts and trips around the world. I attend the same parties as Edwin now, so I don't need to marry him to gain access. Not to mention, it's already part of our marriage contract that our bank accounts never merge. What is his will remain his and what is mine remains mine. What I give Edwin is an equal partnership. Sophie is only another expense."

"A partnership? You make marriage sound like a business deal, Tottenstinker," Heather snapped. "Nothing more than a cold business deal. Do you know what Sophie has that you never will? Love. She brings true love to Edwin. You bring nothing!"

That much was true. I didn't love Edwin, and I knew he

didn't love me. Normally, I'd walk away, leave them to each other, but Author forbade me.

"You offer him love based solely on looks. A mere bauble to hang on his arm, Sophie, that's what you are. When your looks fade, he'll be with the next, newer model. What talent do you have outside of the bedroom? What assets do you bring to the marriage? I doubt you plan to continue to work. You will allow him to pamper you until he grows tired of carrying you."

"Even if my looks fade, I'll still be a hundred percent more beautiful than you!"

"Then why not give this to me? You can have any man you want, yet you set your sights on my fiancé. All I ever wanted was my Happily Ever After, to walk down the aisle to the man I love and see his face light up at the sight of me." The words were ripped from my soul, and I knew Author didn't care. My pain was nothing here.

Sophie laughed cruelly. "Why? Because I deserve it! No one like you deserves anyone as pure and good as Edwin. I have paid a heavy price, and I deserve my Happily Ever After! Do you know what it's like out there for a woman like me? Blondes are the villain du jour. People think I'm some kind of soulless gold-digger who stands in the way of the true heroine, but it's not so. I am the victim here. I will have my Happily Ever After!"

Our words carried a deeper meaning than what Author meant them. Spoken from the heart, I knew what Sophie was referring to. For a while, meetings like *Author Ruined My Life* and *But I Deserved a Better Story* were overrun by beautiful Characters who found themselves cast as villains. They'd complain that they were the Scary Sue, a two-dimensional character who is there just to show how good and pure the heroine is supposed to be, or a sidekick who settled for someone not as handsome as the hero. It didn't matter if they were normally cast in Stories as the gorgeous heroine ninety-nine times out of a hundred, they all moaned about that one time.

Sophie must be like them. Used to being the heroine, she found herself in a villain's role in a previous Story, and won't let that go. Her pity party grated on my nerves.

"Oh, cry me a river! I had the worst life! Always poor, always bullied, I had to build my empire from the ground up. I worked hard for this, and I will not let some overindulged philandress cheat me from my rightful accolade. All because she was too lazy to move past one little setback as a teenager!"

"Fine, let it be war," said Sophie. It was Sophie in front of me, but I knew Author was backing her. I could see it in her eyes. I had drawn the lines of battle; I was outed as a Character who would fight against our supreme god. I would pay a heavy price; my Pyrrhic victory would weigh heavy on me if I should get out alive.

# Chapter Twenty-One

The real battle began the next day. Lorna, in rare form, printed a story about how I was caught torturing my cats. The pictures were badly photoshopped and happened to be printed right next to a story about how Heather rescued the cats. I called the Cat Camp immediately and discovered the truth. My cats were gone, which meant my production stopped. Tabby Pops Coffee was ruined.

The police refused to help me. They were firmly in Author's pocket. I was told that my cats were safe now that they were out of my devilish grip.

Steven and I rode in silence to work. My mind reeled with how this would affect my employees. I knew Author didn't care, but as long as they were in this Story, I felt responsible for them. I was sure Author wouldn't let them starve or end up on the street, but I feared that they'd all lose their jobs.

"Ms. Tottenstinker? What are we going to do? The news this morning was horrible." Earl ran up to me as soon as I got out of the elevator. His scrawny hands rubbed over and over in agitation. His rat-like nose twitched as he looked at me with such hope in his beady eyes.

"It is horrible. I need to see if I can salvage this. Once I know something, I will make an announcement. Maybe by close today. For now, please try to continue on as you normally would."

Steven and I spent the day going over supplies and fielding calls from my vendors. I lost all my contracts and needed to figure out how to pay off any outstanding debts and still pay the salaries of my employees. I called every pet shelter and pet store to try and get a few cats to replace the ones stolen, but no one would sell to me. It was with sadness that Steven and I came to the conclusion that Tabby Pops would close.

We called a staff meeting an hour before close. All my employees looked scared and only a few looked angry. This was not my usual setting. I never gave such disheartening news before. Normally, I just fired individuals, not lay off a whole company.

"I am sure that you all heard the news. Someone stole all our cats, leaving us with no viable source to produce our merchandise, and no one will sell us more cats to continue our work. We have enough products in the store house to carry out what remaining vendors we have with one last delivery, but nothing beyond that. Our bank accounts are mysteriously depleted, giving us little time before we must shut down. The police refuse to help us, and chances of me getting our cats back are slim."

"What will become of us?" asked a female employee.

"I have no choice but to close Tabby Pops Coffee and the Cat Camp. I will have only essentials come in until the final closing to assist with moving merchandising and the final locking of Tabby Pops Coffee. For the rest of you, I'm afraid I will have to let you go. Tomorrow will be the last day for all non-essential staff."

The room erupted with protests. How could I just close the office? What will they do? Where will they go? Who will pay their bills?

Earl spoke up. "What are we supposed to do once this place closes?"

"I don't know. I'm out of a job just as you are. I sincerely hope we can get our cats back and reopen Tabby Pops, but this might be forever. The best I can say is to look for a new job. I will, if contacted, give a good reference for each and every one of you. It truly saddens me to see you all go."

"What if you reopen? Should we go find new job, just to have you expect us to waltz out and work for you?" came an angry question from the back.

"No. Should I get to reopen, if it's feasible for you to return, I hope you will. You will all have a job at Tabby Pops Coffee."

"This is your fault! If you hadn't been a horrible person, we'd still have jobs!"

"No it's not! She can't help it if the cats were stolen!"

The grumbles of my employees broke out into a verbal fight as those who blamed me were met with those who were still on my side.

"Enough!" I put an end to the bickering. "I want only warehouse and distribution to come in next week. The rest of you, start the packing procedures. I calculated that I have enough to pay all of you a full paycheck. You'll get that whether or not you decide to come in tomorrow. This is all I can do for you. I wish I could do more, but we know our free will is an illusion, and we dance for Author. If I can get Tabby Pops back, I will."

Steven and I took home files and started a database of all my employees. If I got Tabby Pops back, I wanted to call everyone personally and invite them back. I hated that this was my fault. If I hadn't stood up to Sophie, would I have lost everything?

For the next week, I worked at closing Tabby Pops. My

entire product was pushed out of the warehouses by Tuesday and my distribution team got the rest of the week off. By Friday, I was ready to close my doors for good. Through it all, Edwin never called me. I wasn't expecting him to suddenly try to help me, but he acted as if he truly didn't care.

"Should I cancel all my wedding vendors?" I asked Steven once Tabby Pops was no more. We were sitting in my apartment with Diamond wrapped around my legs and Chinese food opened between us. "I doubt the wedding will take place now."

"You have only five more months left. Stick it out. Who knows, this could be a False Victory and you'll bounce back." Steven picked up a take-out box of beef with black mushrooms and, using his chopsticks, dished out a portion on his plate.

"I'm the villain. My False Victory would be Edwin leaving Sophie."

"Well, you know how the Story goes: the hero and heroine are lulled into a false sense of security. This can be it. And then you bounce back. We know that will happen. It would be more dramatic for Sophie to interrupt the wedding than for her to just get what she wants."

I dished out a small box of rice on my plate and covered it with a serving of lemongrass chicken with vegetables. "I don't know. Either I need to get Tabby Pops back, or Edwin needs to make a gesture that my new money-less status doesn't bother him for the wedding to continue. As it is, I foresee an end to my wedding."

"See if you can put it on hold? Just in case."

I reached for my phone when it started to ring. Surprised, I quickly picked it up, hoping it was Edwin.

"Well, well, Tottenstinker. How the mighty have fallen." It was Heather. "What was it you said before? You don't need Edwin's money? I guess you do now."

"Where are my cats?"

"They're safe."

"This is just a small bump in the road," I said. "I will get my cats back, I will resurrect Tabby Pops, and I will make Sophie's Happily Ever After as hard to obtain as possible."

"You sound so sure of yourself. Don't forget, Sophie has Author on her side. You have nothing."

"I've played this part many times. I am a born villain, from a family line of villains. If there is one thing I know, it's how the Story arc will once again move in my favor. You are celebrating a False Victory. We all know the wedding is the climax of the Story, and I will be the first bride down the aisle."

Heather snorted. "You'll fail. It's Sophie who will marry Edwin. If you're lucky, you'll live at the end, but you won't get any kind of Happily Ever After."

"And what's it to you? We know Sophie will be the final bride, I don't deny that. But what do you get as her friend? What rewards will be yours other than being cast as Sophie's sycophant sidekick?"

"I get to see you suffer! You don't remember me, do you Rhyna Poisonheart? You ruined my life!"

Steven, who obviously can hear Heather, paused in his eating to look at me. "Poisonheart," he whispered.

"Later," I mouthed before turning my attention back to my phone. "It's been a while Princess Luna Trinity Sunrise Sparkle. How has life treated you since you rode off in the sunset with Prince McHottie? I ran into him before this Story.

He's only become even more handsome."

"You stole him from me! You evil old witch!"

"The Story ended with you two getting married and me dying from being rolled down a hill in a barrel with nails pounded in to cut and slice me. How did I steal him from you?"

"Afterward, I found Prince McHottie. We got married, but you must have put a spell on him. He couldn't get you out of his mind. He started trying to find you in Outer World. When I left him, he never batted an eye or begged me to stay. And it was all your fault!"

"I had nothing to do with that. I hadn't seen nor spoken to Drake in years until just moments before I was pulled into this Story. That was all your problems, not me."

Heather shrieked. "See! You know his real name! I knew you stole him! Well, this is payback. I get to watch Sophie steal your man away! See how you like it!" She hung up on me and I shook my head. What a delusional fool.

"Okay, you have to tell me the story behind Rhyna Poisonheart and Princess Sparkle," Steven said.

I gave him a quick rundown of the Story. "I can't believe she's still mad about that. She's blaming me for a failed marriage."

Steven shrugged. "Maybe you made an impression on Prince McHottie and he couldn't get you out of his mind?"

"Not in a romantic sense. Trust me, I've seen him. He's gorgeous. He remembered me, but it wasn't some kind of love connection. I'm just someone to talk to." I shrugged. "He's probably remarried, anyway."

But, he asked me to coffee. What if that was something more than just friends? No! I couldn't dream like that. It was no use getting my hopes up for something that would never be, whether in a Story or in Outer World.

"Wow, talk about holding a grudge, though," said Steven. He held up a container. "Do you want the rest of the beef?"

"You go ahead."

With Tabby Pops closed, Steven and I found ourselves with a lot of time on our hands. My world spiraled out of control as people around me jumped ship. My bridesmaids called me up and quit. My wedding photographer quit. I had a hard time holding on to the Tabby Pops building in the hopes I could reopen before the ending. I ended up having to sell the larger business building and keeping the Cat Camp. The money went toward paying my debts.

To make matters worse, Lorna assaulted me daily in the paper as some lazy, homebody who ate bon-bons all day and lived off Edwin's money. This was despite the fact that I never accepted a single penny from Edwin and was doing all I could to save my business.

In the end of July, two weeks after Tabby Pops closed, I caved in on something I swore I'd never do: I went to the Church of the Living Plot. Steven was a member, and he felt I'd find some answers there. I did not believe in the Living Plot. The Plot was a tool of Author's, it did not take a life of its own and weave itself around Characters. It did not try to patch nor create plot holes. We served Author, and the Plot served Author.

To my surprise, when I walked into the meeting room, there were several people already there. Among them was Bob. When he saw me, he smiled and came over, sweeping me up in a huge hug.

"I'm so glad you made it. Welcome."

"I'm glad I came." Looking at him, I couldn't help but smile, too.

He cupped my cheek. "See? When you smile like that, you're beautiful. Don't ever let any Author or Character tell you different."

I blushed. "Stop kidding around."

"I'm not. I don't know how to make you realize that. When the time is right, I will let you know just how beautiful you are."

"Come on, Verucca, you should tell your Story," Steven said, pulling me away from Bob. He brought me up to the front and I felt all eyes on me.

"Hi. Um, in this Story, I'm Verucca Tottenstinker. I'm the main antagonist, the Wrong Woman in this romance. I've always been cast as a villain from my first Story. I've been the evil stepsister, wicked witch, abusive stepmother, and nefarious orphan director. I was told by Author at an early age that I was too ugly to be anything good."

"Was it always that bad?" asked Bob.

"As the Character, yes. But, there were moments when Author moved on and I could be myself. I would find the nearest library and hole myself up in there, reading. Sometimes, another character would join me in those moments of bliss." I smiled. "One of my favorites was a really silly fairytale Story. I was the evil handmaiden who stole the pure princess' spot to marry the handsome prince. While Author was focused on the princess, the prince and I would play chess or read or talk. It was those quiet times I treasured the most."

"What happened in that Story?" asked a woman.

"She was brutally killed," said Bob. He coughed and

looked down. "I've been in a few fairytales myself, so I've seen how the villain is dispatched. If not in an honorable battle with the princess, then the villain is tricked into picking his or her fate."

"I was tricked into saying my fate. Back then, I let Author pick all my words and never fought. But this Story...I'm fighting back. As you've seen, I'm suffering for it. I can last the few months we have left. No matter what is taken, I've endured worse."

"What she's not saying is that we believe she's been touched by the Living Plot," said Steven. "Verucca went on a mission to find out her backstory since it's been hinted at so many times. We knew it was something big. What she found out was that she had a Hero's Past. Author wants her to be one thing, but something else is fighting for her to win. And, my friends, we know that force to be the Plot."

After that, a few other people stood up to tell about how they were saved by the Plot. Times when Author didn't pay attention to the Story and some outside force helped them along. I listened with an open mind at their experiences. Bob was the last to stand.

"As many of you know, I'm the Wrong Man to our beautiful heroine. Luckily, I've mostly been forgotten. Sorry, Verucca, but you are now Author's whipping boy."

"I'm used to it."

"Anyway, I came across the Living Plot a few Stories ago. I was in a paranormal romance, the Alpha of a tribe of werecats. Author of that Story forgot to put in details to our characters until the last minute. The Plot made sure that we had gauze or antiseptic near-by when Author put us in danger and sprung a new flaw on us. My tribe won in the end, but it was no thanks to Author, who forgot to give us the quick healing he expected us to have. We are Characters, but we are not perfect. Author must remember to put in our flaws and abilities or we won't always have them. That was the Plot keeping us alive for Author."

The meeting gave me a lot to think about. Watching Bob talk, I could see the handsome hero he must normally be. Strip away the extra layer of fat this Author gave him and let him keep his short hairstyle; he was a handsome man. Even his eyes were changing, a feature he said Author changed to fit who Bob was. In that room, he looked at me, not with the ordinary brown eyes of Bob Smith, but the strangely familiar blue-green of a hero.

# Chapter Twenty-Two

The next day, Author leveled the final nail in my coffin. My apartment caught fire while I was out looking for a job. I made it back in time to see the firetrucks getting ready to pull away. They told me everything was ruined and I was homeless. Diamond made it out alive, to which I was thrilled. I had to leave her with Steven while I went job hunting that afternoon. By dinner time, I found work with a call center that also agreed to hire Steven.

The call center was not the most fun job I ever had. I wasn't even sure why it existed beyond Author's need to see me punished. For nine hours a day, five days a week, Steven and I sat there and listened to people yell at us over a variety of reasons. I wasn't even sure what kind of company the call center worked for, as I was yelled at for cable TV going out one hour and magazine subscriptions being a scam the next.

Every once in a while, Author remembered that I was supposed to be miserable and force my boss to fire me. I'd pack up and leave until Author moved on, and then go back to work. Each time I did, the call center's purpose changed. I'd go back, and now we were telemarketers who got yelled at for interrupting dinner to see if anyone wanted to change their Internet provider. I'd be fired for a day and come back, and we were selling religious reading material. Fired and back to a new position in some company that hired people to get yelled at as part of stress relief. On and on it went, but at least I got a paycheck for honest work.

Lorna was in heaven, writing stories on Edwin and

Sophie's great romance. Now that I was pretty much out of the picture, they stepped out of the shadows and openly announced they were in love. I wanted to move on, to leave Edwin behind, but there was one tiny hitch I had to fix first.

We were still engaged.

Not once since I found out I was losing Tabby Pops did Edwin talk to me. He never returned any of my calls and was always too busy to see me if I tried to stop by. Because of this, we never officially called our engagement off. I had to fix that so I could move on with my life. I wanted what Bob had, a chance to be myself. Maybe that was the last step and Author would allow me to leave for good?

I still possessed the blackmail contract with me and the manuscript. I made copies of each and took the copies with me when I went to Edwin's apartment. At first, Edwin refused to see me, but when I said I was there to set him free, he allowed me to come on up.

"God, Verucca, you look awful," he said as I entered the apartment. "What have you been doing with yourself? Sleeping on the streets? If you're here for money, forget it."

"I'm not here for anything other than to fix what is wrong," I said. "I firmly believe you want me out of your life for good, and I agree with that. You want to marry Sophie, and I don't plan to stand in your way. The only problem, Edwin, is that we never officially broke off our engagement. I'm here to rectify the situation."

"Don't be so dramatic, Verucca."

"I'm not. I give up, Edwin. You and Sophie win. It's either I step aside and let you two marry in peace, or I am forced to admit that I will be entering a loveless marriage to a man who plans on keeping a mistress on the side. I'm too prideful for that." I pulled out the contract. "First order of business is this thing."

Edwin gasped dramatically. "The contract!"

I calmly pointed out the terms of the contract. "All of this, Edwin, is illegal. I know it, and you know it. And its illegality means it's null and void. I cannot expect you to pay me back the interest. I want to rewrite this contract with our lawyers present with new terms."

"What are you saying?"

"I want the contract to read that you only owe me the original loan, with no interest. And none of this 'marry me or else' garbage. We will meet at your lawyer's office tomorrow morning to go over the final details and draw up a new contract."

I placed the contract down and pulled out the manuscript. "This is yours to keep. It is a small copy of the Story we are in. Don't ask how I got a hold of it, I won't ever tell. But, I think you might want to pay attention to some of what Sophie thinks in this. After all, the only person to know her thoughts is Author, and they are revealing."

The manuscript followed the contract and I now looked Edwin in the eye. "Finally, we are ending our engagement. You don't love me and I don't love you."

Edwin actually looked hurt at this. "You're breaking up with me?"

"You broke up with me the moment you saw Sophie. All I'm doing is making it final." I took off my engagement ring and laid it on top of the papers. "I will see you tomorrow, Edwin. Have a good life."

I left and felt so free. I always thought breaking up with anyone would be devastating, but this was the most uplifting experience of my life. I knew that if I loved Edwin, it would have been harder, but I didn't love him. I wasn't sure when I stopped thinking of him as my Prince Charming, but I felt nothing for him. His good looks didn't affect me anymore.

The next morning, we met at his lawyer's office. This time, I brought the original contract, along with the stipend that if I was not the bride, I didn't have to pay for the wedding. I may not be the rich and powerful Verucca Tottenstinker anymore, but I was still myself, and that person was a shrewd business woman and negotiator. I worked out the new contract to one that satisfied Edwin and myself. He was only required pay back the original one million dollars over a course of fifteen years. There would never be any interest.

"Tell you what," I said, pulling out my receipt book. "If you cover the lawyer's fees, I will consider that part of what you owe me this month."

"I knew you'd try to wiggle out of paying," Edwin jeered.

"Darling, you owe me a million dollars, and your first payment is in a week. Now, if you pay the lawyer's fees of two hundred seventy-five..." I did a quick calculation in my head, "then you will only owe five thousand two hundred eighty-one dollars."

"Hardly a dent," Edwin said.

I shrugged. "That's how it goes. Pay the man and I'll write your receipt for the two hundred seventy-five dollars paid today. And, I'm being really nice, Edwin, by adding your fees in on this. So, think about it, what you would pay the lawyer anyway came out of what you owe me. Anytime we agree on money spent, I will also count that."

"So I suppose I'm going to be forced to take you on dates or buy you things? Is that it?"

"No. I'm not forcing you to do anything. You can just make your monthly payments and we'll call it even."

He paid and I gave him his receipt. We left the office and from that day on, I would get a check from Edwin twice a month.

We were barely out of that first month when Lorna struck again. This time, the article mentioned me in passing. The focus was how Edwin and Sophie wanted to marry, but couldn't because I was being a big meanie and taking all of Edwin's money.

*"We want to marry so badly," Sophie claims, "but we may have to put it off for another year. It's all Tottenstinker's fault. Her greed to get Edwin's money knows no bounds. Not only is she forcing him to pay her blood money, but she canceled all our wedding vendors.*

*Dear Readers, we remember the vile Verucca Tottenstinker, that beast who tortured innocent cats and cruelly tried to ensnare the gentle Edwin Van Der Woody III in a farce of a marriage. Now she is forcing our sweet and gentle Sophie Winslow to set aside her wedding dreams. For shame, Tottenstinker.*

I snorted when I read that. I called all my vendors and canceled. I was not paying for Sophie's wedding. Apparently, doing what any ordinary, rational person would do made me the bad guy. Too bad. I guess rich Edwin will just have to shoulder Sophie's ridiculous wedding himself.

After my second check from Edwin, I met with Bob for lunch. We were now seeing more of each other, and I honestly felt like I was falling in love. Bob was a much better match for me than Edwin. If there was any justice in this Story, I would marry Bob and leave Edwin and Sophie to their own devices.

"So, how's your Happily Ever After coming along," Bob asked as we took a seat in Don Juan DeTaco.

"For me, it's going well. I think I plan on aiming at Reader Redemption."

Bob gave a low whistle. "That's a hard one. You won't know if the Reader likes you until after the book is out. Assuming we don't get shelved."

"I know, but it's worth a shot." I opened the menu. "Oh, and today is on me. Not only did I get paid by Edwin, but I also got my regular paycheck."

"Which one is paying for lunch?"

"Work. Edwin's money goes straight into my Tabby Pops fund. If I ever get to reopen, I'll need money."

"How is that going?"

"Slowly. I can't buy new cats, none of the shelters will so much as let me look at them. I tried to get my buildings back, but the bank, which holds the deed now, is refusing my requests. I may never get to reopen my business, but I want money set aside for when I do. It takes a lot of capital to get something like that off the ground, and I can't afford to rely on the kindness of investors."

We looked over the menus and got our free basket of chips and salsa. After a bit of silence, I ordered a bean and cheese burrito with a side of rice and Bob ordered a Macho taco, stuffed with everything they could think of and topped with guacamole and sour cream.

"Reader Redemption doesn't always come automatically," I said as we waited. "My mother got it, but she waited years."

"Oh? What was the Story?"

I shrugged. "Not sure. I never went looking for it. I mean, how weird is it to read a Story and know who the characters are? Anyway, she was a witch, and I think it ran for more than one book. It was a little before my time, and I remember Dad telling me that Mom went in, and when she came out, she was a little different. All my life, she'd wear an eye patch, obsessed over silver shoes, and feared water. And she thought she had flying monkeys. If I was doing poorly in school, she'd threaten to sic them on me, or she'd forget I was her kid and tell me to "fly" to do her bidding."

"And she got a Reader Redemption?"

"Yeah. A few years back, she had tea with a woman who played her character in some remake of the Story. This one was not as…unfortunate looking as my mom." I took a sip of my water. "Oh, and now that character has green skin. It's a little weird."

Bob laughed. "That can happen."

"And a cousin of mine had a combination of Reader Redemption and Author Redemption."

"That's really rare. I don't think I've met anyone who ever saw an Author Redemption."

"He was in a series, as well. He was only given memories as they pertained to that particular book, and for the most part, often wondered what direction he was going in. He'd start off in each Story feeling like the bad guy, but end up feeling like he wasn't evil. And in the end, Author redeemed him, and almost from the start, the Reader redeemed him. He says the only problem with Reader Redemption is the fanfiction. Sometimes they like to pair him with his underage students."

"Thank Author we don't have to act in fanfiction." Bob smiled. "So, you want a Reader Redemption?"

"Yeah. All I have to do is be myself. I can't imagine Author doesn't know how she's presenting Edwin and Sophie. Surely there will be at least one Reader who will read this Story and say, 'Wow, poor Verucca was treated unfairly'."

Bob took my hand and quickly placed a kiss on my fingers. "If it makes you feel better, I think you're secretly the heroine. At least, you are in my book."

# Planning His Pleasure

Life was finally looking up for Edwin. Not only was he free of that repulsive Verucca Tottenstinker, but he could now plan the perfect wedding with the love of his life: Sophie Winslow. Just thinking about his beautiful blonde lover with her svelte body and utterly kissable lips always put him in a good mood. Nothing, not even Verucca's evil attempt to snatch his money away, could ruin his day. He knew why Verucca picked now to demand that he repay her. Not only was she in dire straits, but she knew that Edwin and Sophie were blissfully happy. Her attempts only put a slight hold on their plans. Nothing would stop him from marrying his lovely Sophie.

Edwin just came from his lawyer where he drafted a new contract that he planned to have delivered to Verucca. Now he only owed her one-tenth his original amount due to the stress and harassment. This news would certainly make Sophie's day, and he planned to take her out to the best restaurant in the whole city to celebrate.

Pushing all thoughts of Verucca from his mind, Edwin smiled as he came to the building that now housed his one true love. Like a fairytale princess, she stayed up at the highest point in the tower.

Walking out of the elevator, he was surprised to see that Sophie wasn't waiting for him and the door to her suite wide open. Hearing feminine giggles, he smiled. Oh, that Sophie. She had her friends over and they must have lost track of time. He could see movement in the penthouse's large kitchen. Making his way silently over, he planned to surprise her.

"He's really taking you on a trip to a secluded private island," Heather asked, her voice hush with awe. "That's so romantic!"

*Edwin smiled. His Sophie must be so excited to go. Listen to her tell her friends of what will be their most romantic adventure yet.*

"Well, not quite," came Sophie's breathless voice. He heard her sigh. "We're supposed to go, but it looks like Tottenstinker is trying to ruin that for us. Edwin warned me that we might not get to see his island for a while. Flying out in a private jet costs more than he can afford while Tottenstinker is holding her greedy hand out."

"I can't believe she won't leave the two of you alone," said Lorna. "It's bad enough she ruined your life in high school, but to continue to ruin your life now, that's just shameful."

"I know," said Sophie. "I do so miss the whirlwind of my early romance with Edwin. Back when he didn't have Tottenstinker trying to rob him blind. I mean, he still treats me, but it's taking a toll on him."

*His beautiful Sophie must have noticed how much stress he was under. That was so like her, always thinking of others.*

"Last week, we were supposed to go out to dinner. He brought me a necklace, and do you know which one he got me? It was a single heart solitaire. I know he loves me, but it looked so dinky next to the ones he bought me before this whole fiasco."

*Edwin frowned. Okay, maybe he wasn't giving her the expensive gifts anymore, but it was the thought that counted, right? He still took her out. He still paid for this penthouse. And he was going to pay for their wedding. The huge, extravagant wedding that Sophie deserved. The wedding that he knew would take a huge chunk in his wallet and was the reason for his creating a new contract with Verucca. Surely she knew that.*

"You're not thinking of leaving him because of Tottenstinker, are you," asked Heather.

"Of course not," Sophie said and Edwin relaxed. "I love him. Just because I miss the luxury of our earlier meetings doesn't mean

*I'm going to leave him. I love him, not his money. I'm not Tottenstinker, after all."*

Lorna said, *"Heather, how is your cat sanctuary coming along?"*

*"Oh, very well. I'm thinking of finding homes for them. They're safer with me than with Tottenstinker. Well, I think a few ran away, but who can tell."*

*"I'm so glad you saved those poor kitties," Sophie said. "I just couldn't bear the thought of them suffering under Tottenstinker's rule."*

Edwin stifled his gasp. All his money problems started the day Verucca lost her cats and her business shut down. Until now, he thought that some nameless, faceless vigilante stole them. He could not believe that his Sophie would be part of the cause.

*"I've got a story to go to print on Tottenstinker tonight," said Lorna. "You and Edwin need money, right? Why can't we just say that Tottenstinker, jealous over the pure love of you and Edwin, cornered you and threatened to take Edwin away? We can do some make up to make it look like you were roughed up and then set up one of those fund-raising sites. People always give money to help the needy. And you and Edwin can afford to go to that private island."*

*"Oh, or better still," added Heather, "you can have an incurable disease. Or, at least one that needs an expensive medical procedure. People donate to those things, too. And I'm sure Edwin would be so kind and caring for you in your time of need."*

*"Gee, girls, let me think on those," said Sophie.*

Edwin heard enough. He felt betrayed. Obviously he did not know Sophie as well as he thought he did. He could live with her being a bit more attached to his money than he would have liked, but he'd gladly shower her with all the treasures of the world. But to find out she was going to bilk the public out of money just because he wasn't giving her presents fast enough? Well, that made him sick to *his stomach.*

*"I have a headline for you," Edwin said and stepped into view. The three girls jumped and looked surprised. Heather and Lorna had the grace to look shamed, but Sophie gave him those doe eyes. Now he wondered if it was all an act.*

*"Edwin, my love. We didn't hear you come in," Sophie said. "Let me finish getting ready."*

*"No, we're not going anywhere. We're through, Sophie. You're not who I believed you to be."*

*"Whatever do you mean?"*

*"The Sophie I love would never dream of lying about being beaten or sick to swindle money from good people. She'd give the shirt off her back to help those in need. What happened to the Sophie who baked cookies and taught ruffians to read? What happened to my angel who loved me for me and not my money? No! I have been betrayed most cruelly! I see now that I fell in love with a false image."*

*Tears sprang to Sophie's crystal blue eyes. "Let me explain, Edwin. You have it all wrong."*

*"I heard it all. Good-bye Sophie." He quickly ran from the penthouse and took the elevator down. In a daze, he drove around the city, unsure of what to do next. His wonderful and pure Sophie betrayed him. She had evil in her heart.*

*He parked his car near one of the city's many parks and got out to walk. Still lost in his thoughts, he heard a woman's laughter. Angered that anyone could be happy when he was in such doldrums, he looked to see who it could be. Surprised, he found himself now watching Verucca. She sat on a park bench with that Bob Smith fellow. With sheer abandon, she laughed at something Bob said. The transformation was amazing. When she was not the ice queen he knew her to be, she was almost pretty.*

Verucca placed a hand on Bob's arm, leaning in to talk to him. Edwin felt jealous that Bob got to see this side of Verucca. And the tender way Bob pushed Verucca's hair back behind her ear? It wasn't fair that his cold-hearted ex and Sophie's abusive ex would somehow find each other and become better people. And worse yet, be happy people.

Bob looked up and saw Edwin approaching them. Bob looked surprised and Verucca, once she saw him, became the ice queen once more. It tore at Edwin's heart to see what was now denied to him.

"Edwin? What are you doing here? I thought you and Sophie were going on some big date," Bob said.

"I need to talk to Verucca. It's important," Edwin said. A crazy idea crept in his mind, fed by his sudden jealous thoughts. He'd never be happy without Sophie, and he didn't want Verucca to be happy either. It wasn't fair. He always assumed that he'd go off and live his happy life with Sophie, and Verucca would remain the ice queen. But, seeing her smile and laugh and being affectionate, he wanted that. He couldn't have Sophie, so he'd settle for a half-life with Verucca.

Bob looked at Verucca, who gave a slight nod. He stood. "Well, I guess I'll go get some bread crumbs for the ducks. Excuse me."

Edwin waited until Bob was gone. Verucca folded her bony arms across her flat chest and watched him. He supposed he earned some of her anger. Now that he really thought about it, he treated her rather horribly.

"I owe you an apology," he said. "I should never have cheated on you with Sophie. And, you were right about her. She lied to me. She was not the person I loved."

Verucca raised one slender eyebrow. How did he not notice that before? She was thin and looked like a half-starved skeleton, yes, but she had wonderful bone structure. He wanted to make her laugh the way Bob just did. He could live a somewhat happy life if he knew how to make his ice queen into the woman he recently witnessed.

Dropping to his knees, he took one of her hands. "Take me back, Verucca. I promise to be better this time around. I want to be a man worthy of you. Please, take me back." He saw her mouth twitch. Was that the start of a smile? "Come to my lawyer's office tomorrow. We can restart the wedding, and it will be the affair you wanted. No more pink and baubles. It will be elegant and a black tie affair. You will have all the control. I promise to make it up to you. Please, believe me."

Without waiting for her answer, for he knew the only answer she could give, he jumped up and pulled her to her feet. He kissed her, trying to be as passionate with her as he once had been with Sophie. He was sure her unresponsive nature was due to her being in shock.

"Until tomorrow," he said. "I will count every moment."

Whistling, he left a shocked Verucca as he went to plan his new life. It may still be a loveless marriage, but he was sure he could live with that.

# Chapter Twenty-Three

"What do you mean you *think* you are re-engaged?" Bob stared at me in total disbelief. I didn't blame him. I was having a hard time processing what happened myself. One moment, Bob and I were having a wonderful time and then Edwin showed up. And now, I think we were engaged again.

"I really don't know what happened," I said. "He came over and knelt as if he were proposing. He kept promising that this time will be different. I couldn't say anything, Bob. I tried to tell him no, that I was happier without him, but Author refused to let me ruin the scene. I think our wedding is back on."

Bob sighed, sitting heavily on the park bench. The bag of bread crumbs dangled listlessly from his fingers. "I was honestly hoping Author forgot about us, that we'd finish the Story in peace. Maybe, you know, we'd have our ride into the sunset."

I sat next to him. "Yeah, I was hoping for the same thing." I patted him on the leg. "I was having a lot of fun talking to you. We know Sophie and Edwin are going to end up together, so why drag us back in?"

"She's dragging you back in. I don't really see Sophie coming to me and begging me to go back to her." Bob looked up at me. "You know, you can still be the heroine. After all, the rich, handsome hero just admitted his mistake and wants to marry you."

I laughed. "Not happening. He's only interested in me because he's upset at Sophie. You'll see. The wedding is the key, and I just know I'm not the one who will be dubbed Mrs. Van Der Woody III."

"What if you are?"

"It's just a Story. Marriages in Stories end when the book ends. Unless there's a sequel. I have no illusions that Edwin will seek me out in Outer World and want to recreate our fantastic wedding." I sighed, realizing a mountain of work was now in front of me. I had to call all my vendors and quickly plan the wedding. It was September, and the wedding was only three and a half months away.

"Truth be told," I said softly, "I would love it if the ending was Edwin and Sophie marries, and you...um..."

Bob smiled. "You and I marry?"

I nodded. "Silly, right?"

"Not at all." He took my hand, rubbing his thumb over my wrist. "I was hoping for the same thing."

We sat in silence for a bit before Bob left. Now that I was thrust back in the Story, I had work to do. I called Steven to let him know the recent development. He was just as unbelieving when he found out Edwin re-proposed. He agreed to look into the Cat Camp and getting the building set up for the reopening of Tabby Pops. After all, if I was going to the evil villain, Verucca Tottenstinker, I felt like I should have my business back.

The next day, I met Edwin at his lawyer's office. Edwin promised that this would all be different, and I had no idea why we needed a lawyer. We already settled the agreement with the loan and Edwin was dead set against a pre-nup. Turned out, he wanted there to be rules and conditions to us marrying. It was all business.

"And, since couples cannot owe each other money, the

payback contract between the two of you is null and void," the lawyer said, pulling me from my thoughts. He droned on and on over what was expected of me for over two hours now while I looked over the paperwork.

"No," I said as I dug out my red pen. "These conditions are unsatisfactory."

"Verucca, don't fight me on everything," Edwin whined.

"I refuse to have this be a repeat of last time, Edwin. You promised it would be different, and that means we are equal partners in everything." I clicked my red pen. "Now, as far as the loan, it was a business deal between Tabby Pops Coffee and Van Der Woody Enterprise. It will be repaid, and we have a contract in place for the million dollar loan. It stays, and it is more than fair. As it stands, Edwin's company doesn't have to pay any interest, and you won't find any bank or business out there who would give you such a deal."

"Actually," said the lawyer, "he doesn't owe you one million dollars. He owes one thousand dollars, and that's been paid. You actually owe him money."

"The loan was a million dollars," I said.

The lawyer handed me a new contract. "For pain and suffering, we figured he only owed you a tenth of the loan."

"Illegal," I said. "You cannot sign a contract without both party members. His contract is null and void and the one we previously signed *together* is the actual contract. It's a million dollars, end of discussion."

I pointed to a long paragraph in the new engagement contract. "And this rule about no contact with any males, it's out. This would make me fire Steven, and I can't do that to him. Not to mention not being allowed to hire back any of my male employees, as they would likely be working in the same building, and thus be inside the radius Edwin has set where no man is allowed to be. It's archaic and ridiculous." I drew a line through it.

"It's because you're a little too chummy with that Bob fellow," Edwin said. He reached over and tucked a strand of my hair behind my ear. "Babe, I want to be the only man in your life you're chummy with."

"Edwin, it works both ways. If I have to hire an all-female staff and be without my friends because of their gender, then the same applies to you. Fire your receptionist and any female at your business and keep an all-male staff. No contact with Sophie or her friends. Would that suit you?"

Edwin balked. "That's...that's just uncalled for, Verucca."

"That rule is out, Edwin. Neither one of us wants to fire our staff."

"Fine," he grumped. "But I don't want to hear about you having secret meetings with Bob."

"As long as you stay away from Sophie, we have a deal."

"I want nothing to do with Sophie," he huffed. He gave me a smile that I knew was meant to melt my heart. "You're the only woman I want."

"All that we have to do now is discuss the wedding. I don't believe we need a lawyer for that," I said. "Edwin, I propose we have that portion of the meeting over lunch."

In the end, Edwin agreed to let me have the wedding of my dreams if I keep the Cathedral. The colors were now black, red, and gold. It would fit the first dress I fell in love with. I made a list of the vendors I needed to call and, by the time Edwin left, felt like I could actually learn to like this Story.

Maybe I was the heroine? I had my False Defeat where it looked like the villain would win, but now I was back on top.

Once I accepted my role as fiancé, my life took an upswing. Mysteriously, my cats were returned to me and I was able to reopen a smaller Tabby Pops Coffee. We were now fully located at the Cat Camp and the cats were our biggest concern, but I was able to fix it so I could get everything working again. Most of my employees returned, even though they had to work in shifts due to the lack of space.

My apartment was not damaged in the fire, and neither was my dress. I moved back in, though after living for a few months in more modest surroundings, now felt like a stranger in my own home.

Oddly, Steven now bore the brunt of Author's anger. His computer continued to be filled with pictures and conversations that were not of his making. Some days it was pornographic, and others hinted at illegal drug activity, and some days it was diamond smuggling.

"I'm not sure what Author has in store, but I can feel she's gearing up for something," Steven said as he went through to delete the new content. "I think I'm a drug lord today. Yesterday I was smuggling diamonds, and the day before that I was selling bootleg movies. If I don't end up in jail by the end of this Story, I'll be surprised."

"Don't let it bother you. Right now you're stuck in a plot hole," I said. "I keep you too overworked for you to be a secret diamond-smuggling drug lord with a bootleg movie business on the side."

Once the news that Edwin and I were back together, the paper ran a story about Sophie. Sophie was now the victim of a mysterious illness that wasn't named and could kill her if she didn't have some over-priced surgery. To make matters worse, Edwin walked out on her when he found out, and I jumped her in an alley and beat her up. She needed money for the surgery and living expenses and set up a fund page.

Edwin, upon reading the article, cried about how he had been deceived. I framed the article and hung it in my office.

# Chapter Twenty-Four

I never worked so fast on anything before in my life. By the end of September, everything was back in order. My wedding cake was now red velvet and the groom cade was that tropical flavor Edwin liked. I hired a photographer, band, and a catering company. I was told several times that they normally had longer to prepare, but I was on a time crunch and didn't really care. I would make this the best wedding I could.

By Halloween, things were back on track. I went to have my bridal portraits taken and meet Edwin for dinner at Ristorante Pui Ricco di Te. I felt like a real bride as I pulled up to the restaurant. When I met Edwin, he glanced down at his watch.

"You're late," he said.

I checked my watch. "I'm five minutes early."

Edwin frowned and sat at the table. "So, I received your pre-nup in the office today. I do not find the terms to my liking."

I hadn't sent him a pre-nup, so it must have been Author. "Did you bring it with you?"

He handed me two papers stapled together. I quickly perused the document, taking the terms in. "Okay, what part don't you agree with," I asked. It looked fairly standard to me. If we divorced due to one of us cheating, the offended party got a majority of shared assets. If we parted on amicable terms, everything was split fifty-fifty.

"I do not like you thinking you can take eighty percent of my wealth."

I looked over the terms again. "It's not eighty percent of all your wealth," I said. "It's shared assets that are created after our union. So, what you bring in the marriage is not eligible. For example, if we decide to move into a new apartment that is not owned by either of us before the wedding, that apartment is up for the eighty/twenty split. But, should we decide to move into one of your many penthouses, then that is your asset and, should we split, would remain in your possession. All in all, it appears to be a reasonable pre-nup. I can see several ways for you to keep your possessions from me in the event of a divorce."

"And why is it if I cheat? None of your examples is of you cheating."

"Because you have a history of running to Sophie behind my back. Of the two of us, I can see you in the arms of another."

"What about Bob? You'd run to him in a heartbeat."

I looked at Edwin as Author moved momentarily on. "Yes, I would. I will level with you, Edwin. I love Bob. If Author wasn't pushing us together, I would have been happy with my low-paying job and tiny apartment and Bob. But, since we are now engaged, I will be as faithful as you."

"What does that mean?"

"Simple, as long as you don't go running to Sophie, I won't go running to Bob." I picked up the menu. "We only have until December, Edwin. Let's try to make this pleasant. What made you want to marry me when you had Sophie? Besides Author."

He shrugged. "You, Verucca. When I saw you that day, you were smiling and looked kind of pretty. I wanted that. I knew if I was engaged to that Verucca, I might have been happy."

"You were engaged to that Verucca, Edwin."

We went back to looking at our menus as Author returned. I ordered a salad with scallops and a hazelnut dressing and roasted squab breast with steamed vegetables and Edwin got the oyster appetizer and lobster paella. When my salad came out, he stared at it forlornly.

"Sophie liked salads," he moaned. "She was a vegetarian and really cared about the poor, helpless animals."

"Edwin, can we please have one meal that doesn't involve Sophie," I said. "Please, just this once."

"You never liked Sophie."

"Not going to argue with you on that point," I said and turned my attention to my salad. Without Sophie messing up my wedding plans, I created my dream wedding in under two months rather than the six months it took her to make her monstrosity of a wedding. Firing her had been a highlight for me.

"You know, Verucca, I was thinking…I don't want a black and red wedding. That's too Gothic. Let's go back to the pink and cream idea."

"No."

"And we should get the flowers Sophie wanted. They would look lovely."

"No."

"She picked the most beautiful songs for us. I think we should get the band to play them."

"No."

Edwin pouted. "You don't want me to have any fun, do you?"

"I don't want Sophie's wedding," I said. "Edwin, you are

with me. Please, act like it!"

"Sophie would never talk to me that way!"

I pulled the engagement ring off and held it out to him. "Do you want to marry me or Sophie? Because, it's no skin off my nose to call it all off now. Make up your mind. I will not play second fiddle to Sophie for the rest of my life. It's me or her, Edwin. Who do you want to be with?"

Edwin pushed my hand back toward me. "I want to be with you, Verucca. Okay, I won't mention Sophie any more tonight."

At that moment, the lights flickered as lightning flashed outside. With the rolling thunder shaking the windows, we couldn't help but look outside to see how bad of a storm just rolled in. I could see the storm raging with sheets of rain obscuring the street, but it wasn't the rain that our eyes now focused on.

"Oh, give me a break," I muttered. At the window, looking like some pathetic Dickens orphan was a sopping wet and miserable Sophie Winslow. Tears and mascara dripped down her cheeks as she stared at us, her pink painted lips trembling. Her blonde hair was a wet mess, giving the appearance of a glamorized drowned rat.

"Sophie," Edwin whispered. When he started to rise from his seat, I quickly grabbed his arm.

"Her or me, Edwin. You run out there to her, and I will call the wedding off. Her or me."

Edwin looked at me and reluctantly sat down. It didn't matter to me, but I was not going to spend my time engaged to someone who didn't want me. The moment he ran to her, I was going to cancel. It wasn't fair to any of us. Frankly, I didn't care if Edwin ended up with Sophie, as long as he didn't drag me along for the ride.

At the window, Sophie started sniffling. A passing car splashed a tidal wave of water on her. Edwin turned to me. "Come on, Verucca. We have to help her."

"She's an adult, Edwin. If she can't figure out how to get out of the rain, that's her problem.

Sophie gave a heart-wrenching cry and ran off. I was glad that scene was over.

"Ma'am, your wine." A waiter came over and placed a wine glass in front of me.

"I didn't order any wine. I am sticking to water tonight."

"It comes with your meal."

I looked at Edwin, but he was still staring at the window in case Sophie returned. I took a sip of my wine and frowned. "It's too sweet."

"Yes ma'am." The waiter walked away.

"Edwin, I'm serious. If you want Sophie, then we're through. It's not a threat. It's not fair to either of us for you to jump between us at a moment's notice. You want Sophie, I will call the engagement off and you can go to her and be as happy as you want. But if you truly want to marry me, than you will stay here with me."

"You're such an ice queen," he grumped.

I took another sip, grimacing at the sweet taste. I didn't want to drink the wine, but Author seemed to think the wine was important. My hand shook with the effort to keep the glass on the table each time Author forced me to take another sip.

"I'm practical, Edwin," I said. "How would you feel if I only talked about Bob? Or if I kept leaving you at a moment's notice to run off with him? Would you really feel like I wanted

~ 200 ~

to be with you?"

"Maybe I really want Sophie."

"Then maybe you should call it off with me and go to her."

Our food arrived and I finished the last of the sweet wine. As I did, I felt a wave of nausea hit. I jumped up and quickly ran to the bathroom, unsure of what was going on. It had to be the wine, but why?

I ended up curled in the corner of the last stall, my head resting against the cold tile wall in between bouts of illness. My body shivered from the cold and trembled with weakness. Whatever was in the wine, it took a toll on me.

I heard laughter coming in from the open bathroom window. "Yeah, she's still in the toilet. She was practically green! Now is your chance." Heather. I should have known with how Author was pushing me to drink the wine that nothing good would come of it.

"The anti-freeze worked like a charm," Heather said. "She'll be too sick to finish the date."

Poisoned! I was thinking it would be another attempt to make me look drunk. Poison was a whole other animal. Anti-freeze contained ethylene glycol and could shut down my organs if I ingested enough. Though, I was sure Author didn't want her precious characters to be murderers, so I was probably in for a night of throwing up and the shakes. Author probably didn't know that anti-freeze could damage my kidneys, lungs, and heart.

"Have fun with Edwin, Sophie. Tell us all about it in the morning."

I could hear Heather walk away as I sat there and waited for my illness to pass. What felt like hours later, I was finally able to stumble out of the bathroom. Edwin left already, not caring to see if I was okay. I knew he went after Sophie. His choice was made.

I paid for the dinner and hailed a cab to take me to a doctor. I was too weak to drive. At least now that Edwin made his choice, I should be free to go back to my semi-background status I held when he was with Sophie before.

# Chapter Twenty-Five

After a week in the hospital, I felt almost as if I were back at square one with Edwin. Sure, he stayed by my side at the hospital while my body healed from the harm that one glass of anti-freeze-spiked wine cost me, but he moaned about Sophie every five minutes. Even after I told the police that I overheard Heather talking about putting the ethanol glycol in my drink, they did nothing. I wasn't sure how Author justified it, but Heather got away with trying to kill me. My only saving grace was that Author wanted me to be sick and not dead.

"Kind of like being in some huge action novel," Bob told me when he came by to visit. "I've been shot, stabbed, and survived explosions that should have killed me because Author said so. Seriously, if Author wants you to live, you can get your head cut off and still be fine."

"Speaking from experience?"

"A friend of mine. His headless corpse walked around the book for a good five pages before Author let him die. He said after a while, the pain went away and it was just boring. He still gets neck pains, though."

I wanted to break up with Edwin, but Author refused to let me. He knew that was the only reason I stayed with him. He ran to Sophie, and that was unforgivable. As long as Author tightened the bonds between us, I could do nothing.

After I got out of the hospital, I went to pick up the marriage license. I had to have them rewrite it, as they put Sophie's name as the bride. My momentary lapse that I might be the secret heroine died at that point. Edwin would never wake up and believe I was the true bride. I was stuck with someone who didn't love me while I watched the man I did love from a distance. I knew this hurt Bob, and we both swore to find a way to meet up after the Story ended.

One month before the wedding, my bridesmaids surprised me with a bachelorette party. Edwin and his small army of groomsmen were flying out to some macho resort, and I knew Sophie was going with him. My bridesmaids insisted on bringing me to a strip club just outside the city. I tried to invite Steven, on the reason that he was my gay best friend, but they wanted girls only.

"I wouldn't have fun away," Steven said. "I'd be thinking about my wife the whole time."

"How is she doing?"

"She can't wait to see me again. She's in another Story right now, so we can't talk when we want to. She said she's in one of those Dystopian Stories that are all the rage. Background character, but it's intense."

The strip club was called The Horny Ram. The inside made me feel like I was in an LSD disco dream as various colored lights swirled and blinded me from time to time. Handsome half-naked men danced on a stage. I was surprised to see a few women up there as well. The bachelorette party was nothing special, as I spent most of the evening in a corner while my bridesmaids enjoyed themselves. I left early, but I doubted anyone noticed.

What felt like the next day, it was time for the wedding. After my boring party at the strip club, problems followed my friends. Steven's computer took on a life of its own and he was convinced that Author thought he was some kind of evil agent, spying on Edwin to gain some kind of business secret.

My driver quit on me the day of the wedding, leaving me to get myself to the Cathedral on time. My bridesmaids took my advice to heart and didn't show up. I dressed myself and did my own hair and make-up. The last thing I put on was the garnet jewelry set Edwin accidently sent me so many months ago.

Two hours to the wedding, I started calling Steven. He should have been there, but he was a no-show. This was unusual. His cell went straight to voicemail each time I called.

An hour and a half to the wedding I noticed that the photographer hadn't shown up. When I called her, she told me she quit. She got a better offer for a wedding happening later in the day.

Forty-five minutes to the wedding and I found out my flowers were never delivered. I was told they couldn't, in good conscious, deliver black and red roses as part of a wedding. I was not getting a refund, though.

Ten minutes to the wedding, someone knocked on my door. I was in the middle of trying to get Steven again, and called out to see if that was him.

"No, it's just me," said Edwin. "Are you ready? I thought we were doing that sappy picture of us touching hands with a door between us so I don't see your wedding dress."

"The photographer quit at the last minute. No pictures, Edwin."

"Wedding starts in nine minutes, Verucca."

"Edwin, is Steven out there? He isn't picking up his phone."

"I'm sure he'll show up eventually," Edwin said. "Just be ready to walk down when the music starts."

Steven never showed up. When the Wedding March started to play and I started my walk down the aisle, I knew he wouldn't make it. Something happened, and he wasn't here. I held my head up as I slowly made my way to my groom. My side of the pews held only a handful of people. There were some of my employees, including Earl and Brittney. Bob sat on my side as well, and he gave me the thumbs up sign.

Edwin's side was, naturally, filled to the brim. There were a lot of people who were brought in as background characters. My traitorous bridesmaids sat on Edwin's side. Heather and Lorna were there, too, but not Sophie.

Sophie, I was sure, would find the most dramatic moment to burst in. She and Edwin would run off into the sunset and have their wonderful life together. The end.

Edwin stood with his small army of groomsmen. His face held a look between bored and horrified as I walked down the aisle. I knew the moment he saw the garnets as he frowned even more. In that moment, I was glad the photographer quit. I didn't want that look to be the picture of "Groom's First Look".

I took my place at the altar after setting my bouquet on a pew. The music stopped and the ceremony started.

"Friends, we are gathered to witness the marriage of this man to this woman," said the priest. His voice boomed through the cavernous Cathedral. "Marriage is a sacred tradition in which two people who love and honor each other pledge to do so forever more before the eyes of God and all those present. Edwin Van Der Woody III and Verucca Tottenstinker bring their unique gifts and talents, united on this day, as they build a life together."

The priest looked at me. "Who so gives this woman away?"

"I give myself," I said. I heard a few snickers on Edwin's side of the Cathedral.

The priest shrugged. He took my hand and placed it under Edwin's hand. "Edwin and Verucca, hand in hand you enter into the sacred contract of marriage. Be firm in your commitment; don't let your grip grow weak. Yet, be flexible as you go through life together." The moment the priest ended his little speech, Edwin snatched his hand back and rubbed it on his pants leg.

"Friends, I have had time to get to know Edwin and Verucca as they sought my advice with this wedding. Edwin is a kind and generous man, who has helped countless others in need. His various charities have brought peace and comfort to many and his tireless pursuit of the next breakthrough has led to the creation of several lifesaving technologies. Edwin is a special man who deserves the best life has to offer. A true man of God's grace. He should have a woman who compliments him and exudes the same charitable nature. A woman who is as beautiful as she is kind, to match the fact that Edwin is as giving as he is handsome. His tenderhearted nature should not be tempered by a sour and cruel person who has no thought of others."

The priest paused for breath and I could see Edwin's pride in his face. His ego was thoroughly stroked. I motioned for the priest to continue.

"Edwin Van Der Woody III will you take Verucca Tottenstinker to be your wife, to live with as friend and helpmate, all the days of your life?"

Edwin glanced at me and then at the doors. He sighed,

watching them as if he expected them to open. When they didn't and the minutes dragged on, I nudged him. "Edwin!"

"What?"

"Answer the man."

He sighed. "I guess I do."

The priest shrugged. "Good as I'll get. Okay, Verucca Tottenstinker, will you take Edwin Van Der Woody III to be your husband, to live with as friend and helpmate, all the days of your life?"

Edwin pleaded with me through his eyes to stop this, but Author wanted us to go on. "Yes."

"The marriage vows that the two of you make shouldn't be taken lightly. Nearly every relationship is tempted by strife, conflict, change...another person. To all those assembled here, if any of you have any reason why these two should not wed, speak now or forever hold your peace."

This would be the dramatic point where I expected Sophie to show up. Edwin and I looked at the doors, but they remained shut. I happened to glance at Bob, but he was being held down in the pew by Lorna and Heather. Heather's hand was clamped around Bob's mouth. There would be no interruptions at this moment.

Irritated that the wedding would still go on, I motioned for the priest to continue.

"If you will give me the rings to be blessed," the priest said. Edwin's best man dug in his pocket to pull them out. What happened next could only happen in the wild imagination of Author as it defied all physics.

The ring slipped from the best man's fingers and bounced on the ground by Edwin's feet. Then, it rolled down the aisle in a straight, uninterrupted line to the end. It finally stopped at the hem of an enormously fluffy and sparkly dress.

"Seriously?" I knew who I was looking at as the owner of the frothy dress bent to pick up the ring, but I couldn't believe my eyes. Not that I wasn't expecting her, but because of the get-up she wore. Seriously?

Dressed in a wedding gown that would only look normal on an animated fairytale princess was Sophie. Her blonde hair was so teased and hairsprayed that it formed a tall, stiff halo around her head, causing the veil to cover it like a shroud in the back. Her face was caked with too much make up to create an angelic look, but ended up looking more like the Bride of Frankenstein. Her dress swallowed her in a mountain of satin and lace, her puffy shoulders nearly as high as her hair and her skirt so fluffed out she created a six-foot radius.

Next to me, Edwin whispered, "Sophie," like she was water in the desert. I, too, felt some relief. At last, the end was in sight.

# Planning His Pleasure

When the ring slipped from his best man's fingers, Edwin saw it as a sign that he and Verucca shouldn't marry. The ring made a tiny 'ping' as it struck the floor and bounced twice before rolling down the aisle. Everyone watched it, and no one tried to stop it. No one wanted to be responsible for this farce of a wedding continuing.

To Edwin's delight and surprise, it stopped in front of a cloud of white lace and satin. His heart beat faster as a dainty gloved hand picked up the ring and he could finally accept what he was seeing.

Standing at the entrance was his angel, his beloved Sophie. It was the transformation of Cinderella from the kitchen maid to a princess. Her hair styled so it floated around her like an ethereal halo, her face made up in delicate pinks and creams to mimic that of an angel, and her dress was fit for a fairy princess. All that satin and lace shimmered as she walked up the aisle, the ring still held pinched in her sweet little hand. This was the bride Edwin waited for.

Next to him, he heard Verucca mutter something, but he could no longer think about that dour old hag. Who wanted the wicked witch when the princess stood before him?

"Oh, Sophie," he whispered, the word radiating from his lips like a prayer.

"Stop the wedding," Sophie demanded. "I have proof, Edwin. You do not need to continue this farce any longer. You've lost, Tottenstinker."

"Who is this woman?" asked the priest in wonderment.

"This is the woman I love with all my heart," Edwin declared. He pushed past Verucca and rushed to Sophie's side. "This is the only woman I would ever love."

"But you are marrying Verucca Tottenstinker. Why would you pledge to marry one woman and love another?"

"Verucca held me under an evil contract," Edwin announced. The room gasped. "I know, my friends. The sheer depravity of that woman knows no bounds. She could not have my love, so she trapped me as surely as if she were a witch from a fairytale. I was her helpless victim. If I didn't marry her, she would take everything I owned, by rights of an illegal contract forged between herself and that weasely assistant of hers. They wrote my name falsely, thus binding me to it."

"Not so," cried Sophie. "I have the contract right here, and my love, you missed the greatest loophole in it. Tottenstinker is not as smart as she likes to imagine herself. She made a classic blunder. I even highlighted it for you."

Edwin took the contract and looked at the yellow highlighted portion. "Oh, my darling, you are a wonder. See," he turned to Verucca, "right here is your mistake. It reads, 'And the party known as Edwin Van Der Woody III shall fulfill his marriage duty by meeting the party known as Verucca Tottenstinker at the altar'. Why, there is no mention of actually having to marry you! I am free!"

He threw the contract in Verucca's face. His black-dressed false bride picked up the contract and, without reading it, sat down in the pew next to her fat slob of a lover, Bob Smith.

"This wedding is over! My money remains my own!" Edwin turned back to Sophie and got down on one knee. "My beloved, my only darling, you saved me on this unholy day. Will you do me the honors of being my true bride?"

"Oh, Edwin, yes! Yes, yes, a million times yes! I will marry you!"

Overjoyed, Edwin jumped up and embraced his angelic Sophie.

The guests burst into applause, with the exception of the black bride and her evil lover. They glared at the happy couple, their dreams of ruining the lives of Edwin and Sophie now ended.

"Tottenstinker," said Sophie, "you are completely finished. All your cats have been rescued and placed in good homes. No more shall they slave for you and your fiendish empire of cat poop coffee."

Verucca lifted one dark eyebrow at the couple. Surely she was trying to save face, as Edwin could see the fear in her eyes. That bitter taste of poverty she had before would be her full-time life now.

"Don't worry about your new found poor status," Sophie said. "You won't have any time to enjoy it. See, thanks to Lorna, you'll get a nice hard bed and three disgusting meals a day behind bars."

"For abusing those poor animals?" asked Bambi.

"For her unethical business practices?" guessed Edwin.

"For her constant and daily threats to my paper?" asked Lorna's boss.

"None of that, I'm afraid. She has a crime far worse! See, they've arrested her partner-in-crime, Steven, just this morning. There is no loyalty among thieves, and he squealed like a pig. Thanks to his confession, Tottenstinker will spend the rest of her life behind bars," said Lorna.

"What did she do," asked Latona.

"Tottenstinker and Steven were involved in an illegal diamond smuggling ring! She used her poor cats and that hideous coffee to transfer diamonds stolen from the mines between herself and evil buyers." Lorna smiled, pleased with herself. "That's how she got to be so rich. We all know no one really drank that disgusting coffee."

A murmur of agreement rose from the guests.

Verucca looked surprised, as if she couldn't believe anyone would discover her secret. Not that it surprised Edwin. He always knew she was evil to the bone.

"Let's get married now," Edwin said, turning back to Sophie. "Let's not let another day pass without us making that great commitment to each other. I want to pledge my life to you, Sophie."

"I hoped you'd say that. I spent most of last night and this morning calling all of Tottenstinker's vendors. They agreed to work for me instead. And they got my wedding colors because black and red is just too depressing."

"I am willing to help," said the priest.

"But not here," said Sophie. "I can't imagine wanting to marry in this gloomy old church. Not when it will remind me of that vile woman."

"Then we will marry at my vineyard. The winter will make you look like a glittering fairy, my love."

"I hoped you'd say that," Sophie said. "I told the caterers and vendors to set up there. I'm so glad we think alike."

"What else are soul mates for?"

Edwin and Sophie held hands and led the procession out of the Cathedral. Everyone followed, eager to see the wedding of the century.

# An Ending

Nearly everyone followed Edwin and Sophie. I stayed behind, positive that if I left this sanctuary, I'd be arrested. I could hold off on that for a while longer, hoping the Story ended before the police could drag me out. Bob stayed with me.

"Well, they don't have any sacramental wine, but they do have a six pack of sacramental beer in the mini-fridge under the altar," he said. "Want one?"

"Sure. It's not like they can arrest me for stealing beer on top of diamond smuggling." I kicked off my shoes and sat on the steps of the altar. All in all, this wasn't as big of a disaster as I feared.

"So, diamond smuggling?" Bob handed me a cold bottle of beer.

"That kind of came out of left field. I mean, we knew Author was planning something, but the horrible secret of Steven's changed often. I think this was just what stuck at the last minute."

"Yeah, that is weird." Bob sat next to me and loosened his tie. I could see that he was slowly returning to his natural form, and that he was a gorgeous man when not under the influence of an Author.

"How do you like your ending?" Bob asked.

I shrugged. "I won't know if I got Reader Redemption until later. It's risky. For all we know *Planning His Pleasure* will get shelved."

Bob laughed. "That was the name of this Story? Oh, God,

that's awful!"

"Yeah. It is kind of bad."

Bob took a sip of his beer. "I have a confession to make."

"Oh?"

"Yeah. I, um, I know who you really are. I knew from the moment I saw you."

"I'm the villain."

"No. I mean, I know who you are, Mildred."

I looked at him. I never used my real name in a Story. I was always my Character, so I knew I never told him that. "How?"

At that moment, the air shimmered and the epilogue started. I rarely made it this far and Bob motioned for me to read our various endings. It was rather expected. Edwin and Sophie lived happily ever after in rich, wedded bliss. Lorna and Heather later found rich husbands of their own. Bob lived alone and poor in a trailer park. I spent the rest of my live alone and poor in jail. Steven served some time and then faded from the Story. Everything all wrapped up in a neat bow.

"Rather anti-climactic," Bob said.

"Yeah. Okay, how did you know my real name?"

Bob smiled. "Can't you tell who I am? Come on, Mildred. Really look."

I moved back slightly and gave him a good look over. It wasn't until I got to his blue-green eyes, the slight dimple on his chin, and the overly-handsome chiseled good looks did I recognize him. "Drake!"

"Yep. Prince McHottie was a Nottie in this Story."

"Oh, God, and Heather was Princess Luna Trinity Sunrise Sparkle. She told me that." All of it came rushing back. "You *married* her!"

He shrugged. "Not one of my finer moments. I was young and stupid. Thing was, I thought it would be a good match, but she wasn't smart. I couldn't have a conversation with her the way I could with you. So, when she left me, I thought about finding you."

"She said I was the cause of your break up."

He blushed. "I might have called your name out in my sleep once or twice. But, she left me for another handsome prince. Actually, she does that a lot. From what I heard, she's on husband number five. Any time she's the heroine in a romance, she hunts down her hero and tries to convince him that they are meant to be."

"She needs help."

"Yeah. Anyway, I found you again. When I first saw you, I knew it was you right away, but I was too shy to talk to you. I watched you for a while and tried to figure out what kind of person you were. Mildred, when you're not in a Story, you shine. You don't let some Author tell you you're ugly. When you walk, you float. I watched you blossom as you talked to your groups in Outer World. I fell in love with you all over again."

"All over again?"

He gave me a shy smile. "I had a crush on you in our Story. That's why I kept going to you. It wasn't just because I was bored, it was because you were interesting and I loved to see you smile and you had this cute way of tucking your hair behind one ear when you were thinking."

"So, you found me…"

"I finally got the courage to talk to you, and Author Called me in this Story. I was upset, thinking you were left behind and probably looking at thin air, wondering when I'd be back. And then I saw that you were in this Story. I wanted to tell you, but then I thought, would you like me if I were Drake or if I were Bob?"

"I like both men because both are you," I said.

"I know."

I smiled. "So, about that coffee you were asking me about, before all of this?"

"Still want to go?"

"I'd love to."

We sat there, holding hands, as the world brightened to white. The Story ended.

# Epilogue

By the time the camera focused in on the words, "Gabbing with Gaby", and the audience was a frenzy of applause and cheers. Two women sat in chairs on the raised dais, waving to the audience. One was a beautiful African-American woman with braided hair and wearing a smart business suit. The other was a slender blonde in a pink suit.

The intro music stopped and the audience calmed down. Gaby, the woman in the dark business suit, held up her microphone. "Welcome back! My next guest is the wildly popular author of *Planning His Pleasure*, a novel of erotic proportions that has sold millions worldwide! She has countless fanclubs and there is even talk of the book being made into a movie, staring heartthrob Javin Lurg. Please welcome to my stage, Lola Peyton!"

The blonde woman waved to the audience. "Thank you, Gaby. I'm so excited to be here."

"So, Lola, your first novel was a huge hit! People everywhere are swooning over the handsome and rich Edwin and the sweet Sophie. I have to ask, how did you come up with the concept for *Planning His Pleasure*?"

Lola giggled. "It's something I've been meaning to write for a long time. I feel like I've always had that story in me. Though, honestly, I started writing it as part of therapy. See, I suffered depression after high school, and my therapist suggested I write down my feelings. I was so embarrassed. Instead of writing about me, I created Sophie and wrote about her instead."

"And from there, you turned it into a novel?"

"Sort of. I saw how bad things were going for Sophie, so I started making good things happen to her. That was my first draft. She got a job as a wedding planner and met Edwin. They fell in love and got married. Well, then I realized I had to flesh it out and that gave me the idea to create Tottenstinker." She giggled again. "I love saying that word. It sounds so dirty and is just perfect for that evil woman."

Gaby nodded. "So, let's talk characters. How did you come up with someone as perfect as Edwin? If this started as a therapy project, did you know the real Edwin?"

"Well, almost. Edwin was based off my high school crush. He was the star quarterback, and just so perfect in every way."

"What happened? Did you two ever date?"

"No. A teacher happened. Ms. Priggley the Piggy. She had it in for me for years. See, she hated cheerleaders, and I was one. She even went as far as to give me detention right before prom so I couldn't go. Her niece, Fat Elsa, danced with my crush and the next thing I know, they're dating. It was a horrible conspiracy that just ruined my high school experience and added to my depression."

"Oh, my. I think I can guess who Tottenstinker was inspired by," said Gaby.

Lola nodded. "Write what you know. Anyway, I poured my heart and soul into that book, so it's really nice to see how appreciated I am."

"And what do you think of the division in the fandoms? Verucca Tottenstinker has fanclubs, readers who think you treated her badly for the sake of treating her badly. Do you think, given who she was inspired by, that you put her through more than her fair share of disasters to get back at your teacher?"

Lola looked surprised. "What? No! Those readers have no idea what they're saying. I bet they're all ugly, anyway. They wanted Sophie to lose because they couldn't stand seeing someone beautiful win, and only rally behind Tottenstinker because she was ugly. I don't need readers who don't understand my genius."

Gaby shrugged. "Some fans feel like she got a raw deal. I've read the flame wars between the ones who back Sophie and the ones who back Verucca. One thing that was pointed out was the diamond smuggling came out of nowhere."

"If you read carefully, you would have caught it."

"What about the fanclubs that are dedicated to shipping Verucca and Bob? Any chance of them getting a book?"

"Ick! No! Tottenstinker clearly stays in prison, a cold and bitter woman who never got over the fact that Sophie won. And Bob lives in a trailer park, poor and alone. He never got over losing Sophie. There is no way those two would ever get together."

"It seemed in the book that Bob and Verucca were growing close."

"I have no idea how that happened, honestly. It was like they had a will and mind of their own. I'd go write a scene and they'd just pop up together." Lola sighed. "It was so annoying."

"Any new books on the horizon?"

"Oh, yes!" Lola smiled. "I'm currently writing one where Heather goes to visit one of Edwin's friends on a horse farm. She's there to help the poor horses, and falls madly in love with Edwin's friend. But the head of the horse farm is an evil, greedy woman who also wants him and will stop at nothing to destroy Heather."

"Sounds exciting."

"It is! I can't wait to finish it."

Gaby turned back to her audience. "Well, that's it for this segment. Thank you, Lola, for coming out. It was a pleasure with you. Up next, four-star chef, Chris Bimbino, will teach us how to make the most delicious meals from what's in our fridge! And everyone in our audience gets a signed copy of *Planning His Pleasure!*"

A note from the Author

A special thanks to all those who helped make this book possible. To my cover artist, Gabriel Pendercast, whose artwork and skills are just amazing. To my editor, Dominique Goodall, whose wise suggestions helped steer this book in the right direction, and who I hope didn't run out of red ink correcting my mistakes. To my beta readers, Norm, Debby, Adele, and Letitia, whose insight tackled problems that escaped my notice.

To all my readers, if I could bother you for a moment of your time now that you've completed reading <u>Verucca Victorious</u>, and ask you for a small favor? Would you please consider writing an online review? For an indie writer such as myself, reviews are the best way I can learn how you feel about my work. I could never make it this far without you, and it is for you that I strive to make each book the best I can produce. If you enjoyed my story, please, tell your friends and leave a review to let me know how you feel. Thank you, from the bottom of my heart.

# Upcoming books

Coming in 2016
Kore, Space Station *Olympus* novel, book 2
*Eighteen years have passed since the birth of Kore, daughter of Demeter. She's ready to take her rightful place as Goddess of the New Spring. At her coming out party, she meets the most fascinating man, one who captures her heart with one glance of his sad, dark eyes. He gifts her with a small necklace with a ruby pomegranate charm. This man is Hades, Lord of the Underworld. A man she was raised to fear.*

*For eighteen years, Hades waited for Kore to come to age. Persephone has gone into a Stasis Pod, waiting for her next host. He knows his time is limited to convince Kore to become the next Persephone. Demeter tries to thwart him at every step, determined to stop the natural order of things, to bring eternal Summer to Space Station* Olympus. *Without a wife, Hades knows he'll live in eternal torment until the next Kore is picked.*

*Joined by an unlikely group of allies, Hades woos Kore away from the safety of her mother and into the depths of the Underworld. When Demeter finds out, she makes the entire Station suffer in grief with her. Can Hades convince Kore to be his wife before all life on Space Station* Olympus *dies?*

Coming in 2017
Forbidden Magic
*In the land of the ten kingdoms, everyone knows of the strife between the kingdoms of Anstaria and Fanarias. Deep hatred festers between them ever since the Magus War many hundreds of years ago. Some say the hate runs because of the overspill of magic that coated both the kingdoms after the war. Where Fanarias was blessed by the wild magic as herds of horses mutated into graceful unicorns, Anstaria was cursed as flocks of birds transformed into carnivorous beasts. Other say the hate and mistrust is over the subject of magic; Anstaria relies more on science and has banished magic forever, while Fanarias thrives on power.*

*For any reason, when Anstarian princess Dionne is a young girl, the two kingdoms try once more to barter for peace. An innocent flirtation turns the head of Fanarian prince Lias, but neither kingdom is ready for that kind of joining. Lias, torn form whom he believes to be his soul mate, vows to not rest until she is his. Dionne, blissfully unaware of the conflict, is betrothed to a high-ranking duke of another kingdom.*

*War comes to the ten kingdoms as Fanarias rages against Anstaria. Magical plagues and mysteriously powerful knights tip the war in favor of Fanarias. Dionne, raised to hate and fear magic, becomes what she fears the most when an accidental burst of magic saves her life. Seen by the enemy, someone blackmails her into joining the war on the Fanarian side.*

*If she disobeys, she can be executed as a spy or a witch. If she obeys, she betrays all she loves. Caught in the horrible claws of war, Dionne must decide her path as Fanarian troops march ever closer.*